499

DON'T MESS WITH TESS!
Praise for the Tess Camillo series by Morgan Hunt

"Sticky Fingers . . . is fast-moving and clever, raunchy and sexy, serious and funny; a delight to read."
—Marianne Moskowitz, *WomanSource Rising*

". . . an engaging tale of equal parts murder, sharp dialogue, loss, and humor."
—Chelsea Fine, *Just Out*

"You will be fooled, which is half the fun of reading a mystery. Morgan Hunt gets better and better as a writer. Three cheers."
—Rita Mae Brown, *New York Times* best-selling author

". . . Hunt's character development is so flawless you'll think she's been writing Tess Camillo mysteries for years. With style, wit, and an irrepressible sense of humor, Hunt draws you into the story and doesn't let go until the last word . . . and then leaves you wishing for more."
—LaRita M. Heet, Editor-in-Chief, *Jane* and *Jane Magazine*

"This is a terrific amateur sleuth tale. . . . "
—*The Mystery Gazette*

"Glib, funny, heart-warming, and heartbreaking, Hunt pulls the strings and has . . . (the) reader thoroughly absorbed in Tess' life and antics before we can say 'snake-bite'. . . . Funny, colorful, quirky, and an absolute delight to read!"
—Alex Wolfe, *Kissed by Venus*

"Morgan Hunt's familiarity with breast cancer shows in the sensitivity, fear, strength, and dignity that she gives to Tess throughout her ordeal. . . . (the author has) a wonderful sense of humor which comes through again and again; a great book."
—Cherie Fisher, *Reader Views*

"Tess narrates with verve . . . an engaging swift read."
—Ethan Boatner for *Lavender Magazine*

"It's a genuine pleasure to read a mystery with smart writing. Morgan Hunt immediately captured my attention and made me shiver until learning the startling truth. I can't wait to read her next book."
—J. Miyoko Hensley, writer, *Murder She Wrote*

*To Dede—
A friend of my
heart and an extremely
talented writer —*

FOOL ON THE HILL

A TESS CAMILLO MYSTERY

Morgan Hunt

4/2/08

MORGAN HUNT

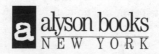

alyson books
NEW YORK

Manufactured in the United States of America

Published by Alyson Books
245 West 17th Street, New York, NY 10011
Distribution in the United Kingdom by Turnaround Publisher Services Ltd.
Unit 3, Olympia Trading Estate, Coburg Road, Wood Green
London N22 6TZ England

First Edition: April 2008

08 09 10 11 12 13 14 15 16 17 a 10 9 8 7 6 5 4 3 2 1

ISBN: 1-59350-027-0
ISBN-13: 978-1-59350-027-6

Library of Congress Cataloging-in-Publication data are on file.

Cover design by Victor Mingovits

For Kate Mattes, who gave the gift of hope;
and for my family—Jeff, Mom,
Tom, Debbie, J.D., and Kim.

Blood runs thicker than printer's ink,
and the love that bonds our unique brood
runs deeper than either.

ACKNOWLEDGMENTS

Special thanks to: Rebecca Cabigao, Damian Gahagan, Alan Garay, M.D., Richard "Hardcase" Hubbard, my editor Joe Pittman, and to my Beta Readers: Maggie Thompson, Fran Brass, Alison Thomason, Glenna Lang, Tamar Berg, Arvinder Dhillon, and Judy Baker.

1

THUNDERSTORMS AND OTHER MOIST ENCOUNTERS

THE STARS ARE SO FAR above the earth that we're usually oblivious to what's going on up there. While we brush our hair, comets dart through galaxies and sunspots dance into inky space. We grow bored in grocery lines as meteor showers sparkle and novas burst on the scene. We rarely know when we're being star-crossed.

But that captivating spring Saturday night, I knew one star would cross my path: I had primo tickets to a Gabrielle Leatheross concert! I'd soon hear the lovely growl and fiery riffs that gained her popularity not only with fellow lesbians but among rock lovers everywhere.

I picked up no negative vibes before the concert, no evil feelings at all. Oh, I had odd feelings. At least that's what some folks would say about a lesbian still living with a straight housemate she once had an affair with. Odd would be a kind word.

It's not that I haven't had honest to goodness lesbian romances. It's not that Lana hasn't been involved with men and still dates whenever she meets a decent prospect.

It's that we're true friends. We know each other's third grade teachers, ATM codes, breakfast food preferences, and birthmarks. We care more deeply than hormones run.

It's that San Diego is more affordable when housing costs are shared.

It's that nothing better has worked out long-term for either one of us. And it's the memory of an animal passion that used to course just below the surface of everything we did or said.

Eighty-twelve years ago, we'd hooked up when Lana was flirting with bisexuality. We entertained each other in bed and out for almost two years. Then, while waiting in line at her credit union, she connected with an unusually beautiful man, both a poet and a boxer, and decided that she had, after all, only been flirting.

Unlike many women my age who complain of diminished hormones, I am as sexually interested as a sailor on shore leave. And every once in a while, the sub of sexual tension between Lana and me raises its periscope, searching for trouble. Because I really do care for her, I keep all hands on deck.

I checked out my image in my bedroom mirror. The black boots and jeans looked right, but the red pullover didn't work.

I yanked a loose fitting white pirate-style shirt from a hanger and put it on. Loose fitting is important, because a while ago, my trans-abdominal rectus muscle bought a condo in my left breast: belly now resides where boob used to be. My ankle bone may still be connected to my leg bone, but my belly button has been re-sected; some innards turned outward, and my nerves have undergone numerous nasties, leaving strangely numb nether regions on the front half of me.

But it was better than dying of advanced invasive breast cancer.

With a large aggressive tumor, there was little rational dispute about the mastectomy, but I did have choices about replacing the breast. Lately, prosthetics have come out of the closet. I saw Minnie Driver pull the artificial arm off a TV character the same night Heather Mills and her artificial leg danced with the stars. This liberation is particularly good for Iraq war vets returning with fewer body parts than they left with. But the same puckish deity who designed scrotums graced me with fulsome curves. For me, a breast prosthesis would have had to be sizable. If I didn't wear any prosthesis (a perfectly reasonable option taken by many survivor sisters), I'd have gone through life lopsided. Doctors warned this would not be good for my body mechanics. Given my choices, I opted for breast reconstruction from my own abdominal tissue. With the help of talented surgeons, the result is a left breast that's a slightly smaller than my right, an incision scar where the nipple used to be, and a big slash across my lower belly. Not bad, compared to a coffin.

The pirate shirt worked. I checked my mirror again, more pleased with what I saw. It's taken me a while, but I genuinely like the face in the mirror. I look like someone you've met before. My familiar face, high brow, and large brown eyes have inspired comparisons with everyone from "cousin Rachel" to Isabella Rossellini. I'm a stocky size 16, however, which might insult Isabella.

I put the concert tickets in my wallet, opened my bedroom door, and went to see if Lana was making progress.

I immediately stumbled over Pookie, Lana's dachshund. This dog could play either lead in *Dumb and Dumber*. Naturally, Lana loves her dearly. Probably because I merely tolerate Pookie, the dachsie follows me everywhere, tripping me on a regular basis. Raj, my honorable Welsh terrier, makes the rounds of his territory, not needing to be constantly underfoot. When it comes to Life, Raj gets it. He's the most vital soul I know.

Lana's bedroom and mine are situated at opposite ends of a hallway with a bathroom in between. Her bedroom is at the north end of the colorful Guatemalan rug that runs the length of the hall. I knocked on her door. "Seven-thirty; the show starts in an hour. Need help with anything?"

Both Einstein and Lana perceive time the same way—a flowing, relative dimension. With Lana, it's not the deliberate feminine power ploy that some women use to keep people waiting; it's that she's so non-linear she attains every goal by a circuitous route, a route that might in the middle of dressing involve watering the plants, checking her supply of ginseng, or sketching in her journal; a route that makes us ten to sixty minutes late wherever we go.

She let me in and walked over to her dresser. Lana was jazzed about catching Gabrielle's opening act, Cody Crowne, an older rock star she'd been enamored of as long as I'd known her. That must've motivated a focused effort because she looked almost ready.

"Have you seen my silver watch?" Lana temporarily misplaces objects on a routine basis, one of her less endearing traits. Her back was toward me, so I saw tousled blond hair against an aqua blue sweatshirt, with blue jeans hugging her frame. But no silver watch. I scanned her room once briefly. How anyone could find anything in the chaos of clothes, plants, pillows, shoes, jewelry, candles, mail, newspapers, and miscellany was beyond me.

"No clue," I replied.

She turned around. Lana Maki's Finn forebears had obviously known some Lapps, or Samis, as those indigenous people are sometimes called. In her, these unique genetics produced astonishing blue eyes with an Asian epicanthic fold and high cheekbones that simultaneously contradict yet fit the rest of her Scandinavian looks. She really knew how to use those eyes. "Oh, who cares about the watch," she said. "Let's go!"

I fought to hide my grin.

Moments later we were on our way, scooting west down the Washington Street hill, merging onto San Diego's I-5 freeway, heading for the downtown Embarcadero with its open-air arena.

San Diego is eye candy by day or night. It has all the beauty and allure of a tropical paradise with minimal bugs or humidity. Over two million people have discovered those virtues, so it also has congested traffic. As I geared up my silver Infiniti FX, we passed starlight rippling on the bay, queen palms swaying, and more than a few slow-poke drivers.

At the Embarcadero, we paid the rough equivalent of the Crusaders' ransom for Richard the Lion-hearted as a parking fee, then threaded our way through the crowd to our seats. Seats, of course, were superfluous. Everyone was standing. The audience was mostly lesbian, with some straight couples mixed in, along with a few single men, apparently content with whatever action might (or might not) come their way.

I hugged Joy and Phyl; waved to Marisa and Page; high-fived Tina and Sandy, all the time weaving Lana protectively through the crowd.

"People think we're together, don't they?" Lana asked.

"I hope not; I'm cruising," I teased. The part of me that really was cruising found it quite pleasurable—so pleasurable I don't even remember when Cody Crowne was introduced.

Next thing I knew, he was up there, leading the crowd in a song from the 80's. Back then, if bad boy rock appealed you listened to Springsteen or Cougar. If you wanted a side order of Detroit with your bad boy rock, you went with Bob Seger. And if you really wanted a folkie in rock clothing, your choice was Cody Crowne.

"I'm missing my tips; I'm longing for sips / But bear the cross I must / I gaze out to sea / Weigh the penalty / For it's C and S or bust," Cody sang the ballad of some lost soul's struggle to get clean and sober.

I studied him to see if I could discern the reasons for Lana's attraction to him. For a rock star, he was noticeably well-groomed. He had shiny brown hair, gray at the temples, and a trim goatee. His skin was bronze, as if he spent his life roping cattle instead of recording music. A creamy linen shirt, cinnamon suede pants, and dark Frye's boots completed his outfit. With his soulful eyes, he looked like a cross between Lord Byron and Tim McGraw.

Gazing at Cody, Lana shivered with delight. "Thanks so much for this!" she told me, then leaned her lips close to my ear. "I can still remember when he first released the Bayberry album—my boyfriend and I played it the night I lost my virginity. I memorized every song; every line. Oh, Tess, I've always wanted to see him in concert, but it never worked out. Now . . ." Her eyes drifted back to the stage.

"You took me down to the wire / Fueled by my fire / Left me more alive and a-loved," Cody repeated the refrain to his

final number. He took his bows, and the show broke for intermission.

Lana and I indulged in Michelobs and popcorn from a vendor who apparently took capitalism lessons from the parking folks. As we waited for the main attraction, a skinny black sister in the row behind me tapped me on the shoulder. "It's on the news: A young okapi just escaped from the zoo. Anyone who's driving back on 163 tonight—watch for the okapi! Pass it along."

I did so, passing the road kill bulletin along to Iris, a dyke on my right who looked like she could tenderize steak with her bare hands.

"What the hell's an okapi?" she asked.

"It looks like a cross between an antelope, a giraffe, and a zebra," I told her. I'd seen the strange but beautiful critters at the zoo and Wild Animal Park many times.

Suddenly Gabrielle stole everyone's attention. In a maroon leather vest and silver jeans, she belted, snarled, and purred, luring us into a realm of faithless lovers, wild horses, thunderstorms, and other moist encounters. Soon, nothing else existed but Gabrielle Leatheross, her voice, and her guitar on the stage of the San Diego Embarcadero.

The one time I looked away to check on Lana, her eyes were riveted on Cody, who watched Gabrielle from the wing. Even he seemed transported by Gabrielle's grit and glory.

Inhaling the elated atmosphere, we never caught the scent of abject cruelty also blowing on the night's breeze.

2

DARK DEEDS

HE ZIPPED AND FLUSHED, *then turned toward the sink to wash his hands. His peripheral vision caught something behind him. Before he could turn around, a sharp pain in the back of his head eclipsed his efforts. He sank toward the floor. Strong arms broke his fall.*

"Good night, Gracie," came a whispered growl.

Through the ache and confusion, he felt tape across his mouth.

"Move it!" a voice urged.

Someone put an arm around his shoulders, leaned into him, and chatted about the Padres as though they were old friends, supporting him while they walked. The voice seemed vaguely familiar, like he would recognize it if his head would just stop pounding.

He was maneuvered to where the vehicle and all necessary equipment waited. He felt himself being shoved onto a hard floor. Someone tied his hands and feet. Suddenly a blindfold impeded his already pain-blurred vision. He heard a door slam and an engine start.

After a considerable ride, the vehicle pulled over and the engine quieted. He shook from the slam of a door. Footsteps approached. Someone opened a hatch or window; he felt the cool night air. He could hear people talking but couldn't tell what they were saying. His cheek brushed up against some boards; he smelled freshly cut lumber.

The voices approached again. In a moment, they were upon him, lifting his body on top of the boards. His bonds were loosened. He mumbled thanks through the tape, but his relief was temporary as his arms and feet were soon re-bound to what felt like scaffolding.

His legs cramped. He tried to find a more comfortable position but received a kick so powerful it ruptured his spleen.

"You are one sick bastard. I better never hear another word about owing you as long as I live," one of them said in a threatening tone.

"I've waited years; let me enjoy myself," the familiar voice tittered.

In the background, he could detect the sounds of traffic; nearby, the clink of metal tools. Suddenly, nothing registered but the most bone crunching agony.

3

FOOL ON THE HILL

IT'S PROBABLY A THROWBACK to childhood when it meant church and Mickey D's, but when Sunday dawns, it feels different to me—sanctified with a quiet grace and leisure the world could use more of. Most Sundays, I rise early, retrieve the newspaper, and then bask in our breakfast nook with the crossword and comics until Lana joins me for brunch.

This morning, however, I woke up restless. An overcast haze—what local meteorologists call the marine layer—blocked the sun. In a few hours, the sky would be spit-shined, but for now, the weather was cool and moody.

I put fresh water out for the critters, brewed some java, and flipped two eggs over easy, trying to keep the kitchen noise to a minimum while Lana slept. If I wake her on Sundays before she's ready, she can be as prickly as the cactus in nearby Borrego Desert.

I closed the Jamaican Blue coffee beans and returned them to the freezer, tucking them between a bag of Kona Gold and one of Guatemalan Supreme. I'm beginning to think all the nickel bag dealers of the 70's have gone into coffee marketing. The older I get, the less certain I am whether Simple Pleasures should be served in a mug or a bong.

Sipping the aromatic brew, I decided this cool, quiet Palm Sunday morning would be ideal for a hike, and I knew just where I wanted to go.

Heading north on Interstate 5, there was little traffic at that hour. Get behind the wheel of a competent car on an uneventful drive, and the mind cruises too. Next thing you know, you've traveled thirteen miles and you've covered topics like how much butter to put on microwave popcorn without getting it too greasy, whether to code your new project in CGI or Perl, and why songs pop into our heads at odd moments and refuse to leave.

Some part of my forebrain still focused on driving, though, because I didn't miss my exit. Carmel Valley Road, which forms the northerly boundary of the Los Penasquitos Marsh, curves like an inviting woman. No wonder I enjoy it. On a good day you can spot egrets, grebes, mallards, coots, and the occasional great blue heron among the reeds. I took my time, having a Zen moment with these creatures who don't give a honk about the stock market or politics.

At road's end, I turned south along Torrey Pines Beach and caught a view as fine as any on the Riviera. Miles of splendid coastline hosted San Diego's hang glider port, Black's Beach (shrine to Our Bum of Perpetual Nudity), fairways for the rich and famous, and closest to me, Torrey Pines State Preserve.

I took the Preserve turn off and pulled up to the ranger station to pay my parking fee. No ranger was in sight. I checked the car clock—8:03 a.m.

I got out and stretched, figuring the ranger was running late. I heard a shuffle. Up ahead a young man in uniform was fussing with a swung-open metal gate. A Jeep bearing the Preserve logo was parked nearby. I moseyed over to make my presence known.

Blond, fit, and definitely young, he sported a fuzz mustache and a badge declaring him Ian Coley. "Pardon me, Ma'am. I didn't hear you pull up," he offered.

I just love it when youth call me Ma'am. It makes me want to light a joint right then and there, toke deeply, and castigate, "Who you calling 'Ma'am?' I groove to 91X. I love caressing leather and licking butterscotch off soft skin. I'm wildly youthful at heart." Instead I responded, "I just got here. What's going on?"

"Checking things out. Someone cut the padlocks on the gates again last night. Thought I'd be finished before anyone showed up."

"People go through that much trouble to avoid a two-buck parking fee? Bolt cutters would cost more than that."

"Happens every so often." He wiped the sea damp from his face and walked with me back to his station. "The Preserve's pretty vulnerable at night. People running drugs or illegal immigrants—if they pull boats up on this beach, no one's gonna see them. After dark, there's not much happening, people-wise, between La Jolla and Del Mar along the coast."

"You guys don't have a night watchman or night ranger, whatever they're called?" My inquiring mind wanted to know.

"Not in the budget." He smiled ingratiatingly and I could see how he must have broken hearts at the prom, possibly as little as a year ago. "That'll be two dollars."

I exchanged two bills for an Admit One ticket and snippet

of masking tape to affix it to my window, making it legal for me to park at the Preserve all day if I felt like it.

I followed the winding road into the park, climbing the steep rise, loving how my Silver Bullet hugged the road. At the crest of the hill, I pulled into the empty parking lot. To my left was a modest adobe museum, crammed with displays and lore on featured flora, fauna, and—of course—the rare *Pinus Torreyana*. To my far right were rest rooms. The museum didn't open until nine, which was fine with me. I wanted solitude.

Just then a Buick pulled into the lot. From it emerged four women with the cliquish air of nuns or birdwatchers. Most visitors to the Preserve come for the hiking trails that wind down through high desert landscape, past honeycombed sandstone cliffs, all the way to the white beach below. Apparently the birdwatcher-nuns wanted solitude as much as I did, for they backtracked down the road toward the beginner's route, the Guy Fleming Trail, a loop with diverse scenery and adequate views.

I chose the more rigorous Razor Point Trail—not the most difficult the Preserve offers, but challenging enough. Much as I'd like to think of myself as incredibly daring, the reality of having to lug my extra pounds against gravity on the return climb was enough to dissuade me from X-treme hikes. Besides, Razor Point Trail *sounded* adventurous.

The sun was trying to clear the marine layer, resulting in a sky that looked like a molting animal, partly this and partly that. I took off down the soft dirt trail, inhaling the piquancy of sage and pine. Some exercise exhausts; some revitalizes. This hike was already doing me good.

While sage predominated, ground pinks, chemise, lupine, popcorn flower, and miner's lettuce laced my path, and every so often a tall red monkey flower poked up through the chaparral.

To my right, a sandstone escarpment rose from the sea, pocked with random holes for which geologists would have logical explanations, but which to me looked like the cubby holes we had in kindergarten. If someone poked around in them, maybe she'd find graham crackers, milk, and crayons.

My neck and shoulder muscles, which get tense from computer work, loosened. I breathed more deeply and couldn't help smiling. Down, down, down curled the trail; up, up, up went my spirits. Along the way, I watched for the truant okapi. Couldn't hurt.

By the time I reached the second vista deck and stopped to take in the view, I was high. Not on Acapulco Gold, not on Jamaican Blue, but on life itself.

I paused again at the bottom of the trail to enjoy the Pacific, then turned back for the uphill jaunt. Three or four minutes from the top of the hill, I was huffing a bit from the climb when I heard ravens squawking. My gaze followed them, to see what all the excitement was about.

My heart jackhammered.

About 120 feet to my left, and maybe 30 feet above me, over the side of a gravel-capped cliff facing the Pacific, hung a cross. With a man on it. Crucified.

Thick ropes under the cross bar of the crucifix were secured to a cement park bench at the cliff edge, effectively suspending the cross over the cliff.

Adrenaline hit me like a Red Bull with an espresso chaser. What could it really be? Today was Palm Sunday, not Easter. But the Greek Orthodox Christmas is different from mainstream Christianity's; maybe it was a mannequin used for some sect's Good Friday rite. Maybe Mel Gibson was filming a *Passion* sequel.

I huffed hard as I scampered up the remainder of the trail and across the parking lot. The birdwatcher-nuns' car was gone. Ranger Coley was sweeping the museum entrance when I broke the news to him. To his credit, he dropped the broom pronto and took off for the picnic loop where the park bench was located.

Thoughts spinning, I followed. I told myself over and over that it had to be a prank; that it couldn't be Cody Crowne's body hanging on the cliff. And tried to get the song "Fool on the Hill" out of my mind.

4

A ROACH
IN THE COOKIE JAR

RANGER COLEY RADIOED 911 immediately. I didn't mind
if he called 911 and a half; we could use all the help we could
get. He secured the picnic area and informed the museum staff
of the circumstances.

Two uniforms arrived in less than ten minutes, quickly followed by the Homicide Squad and Crime Scene Unit. Detective Sergeant Rex Gonzalez, handsome enough to star in his
own cop show, was apparently in charge. He ate and moved
constantly, like an ex-smoker with a nicotine jones. "No foot-
prints," he remarked through a mouthful of Cheez-Its to no
one in particular. "They used brush to wipe the ground clean
behind them. And any vehicle tracks have been obliterated, but
we'll find something."

He ordered three other officers to haul the crucifix up the
cliff. They dragged it onto the ground in the picnic area. No
pulse, no breath; Death had long since come and gone. The

body was rigid; the face ashen and anguished. Blood had oozed from his mouth and caked on the goatee. Around his head was a diadem of thorns. The boots were missing, but the shirt and pants looked just like those Cody had worn on stage last night. The wrists were so gruesomely distracting that it took me a few moments to realize that his fingertips had been amputated.

I've seen dead bodies before; you can hardly be a *CSI*, *Bones*, or *Jordan's Crossing* fan without being exposed to battered remains on autopsy tables. I'd helped the police in a murder case last year during which they'd shown me photos of a murder scene. But believe me: photos and TV images don't rivet your soul like an up-close-and-personal corpse. I know that Kinsey Millhone, Sam Spade, and Carlotta Carlyle don't get all woozy when they see a dead body. But they didn't see *this* dead body. And they didn't go to a Bible college.

For two intense, baffling years at Everette Bible Institute, I pursued spiritual knowledge while suppressing my budding lesbianism and doctrinal doubts. I fit like a Bundt cake in a bread pan, but when it came to ancient history, homiletics, eschatology, apologetics, or theology, I learned my stuff. And among the stuff I learned were details about crucifixion.

Many people think a crucified person dies from blood loss of the punctured wrists and feet. (Most crucifixion nails pierced the wrists, not the hands.) At EBI I learned a more hideous truth. The cross bar was positioned in such a way as to strain the rib cage muscles, making it difficult to work the lungs. If the victim raised himself by pushing on the foot crossbar to ease his breathing, the pain in his feet tormented him. When he could no longer tolerate it and let himself slump, he couldn't breathe. The victim struggled between suffocation and excruciating pain until one or the other depleted him. All in all, an execution method that leaves no gray area about "cruel and unusual punishment."

By the time spirits of ammonia had done their job, the area was bound with yellow crime scene tape. The photographer and medical examiner jockeyed for position around the corpse.

Detective Gonzalez directed the CSU to search the park bench and the immediate surroundings. He seemed especially interested in anything that might have clung to the wild buckwheat growing between the park bench and the cliff top where the ropes had been lowered. When the evidence techs had bagged and tagged to his satisfaction, he turned toward me. "Ranger Coley says you recognize the victim?"

I steadied myself. "He's a musician, Cody Crowne. I went to see him in concert last night down at the Embarcadero. He opened for Gabrielle Leatheross."

Gonzalez nodded. "That matches the driver's license we found in his pocket."

The Medical Examiner, a middle-aged woman wearing a silk scarf and cynical weariness, finished scrutinizing the body. She stood up, stretched her back muscles, and looked around. She gave a honeyed bark, "Theo!"

A young evidence tech with two nose piercings zipped his pants and spun toward her. "Ma'am?"

"When you're around me, keep it in your pants. You have to whiz, find a bathroom like the rest of the civilized world." She turned toward Gonzalez. "Time of death would be a few hours after the time of crucifixion, which I'd say was between ten and midnight last night. Several of his teeth are smashed or missing. That's judging from what I can see by pulling his lips back; the jaws are fixed in rigor. Hope you don't need finger-prints or dental records for a firm ID, Rex."

"Removing fingerprints, smashing teeth—an identity dodge. But then . . ." I wondered aloud.

Gonzalez finished my question " . . . Then why leave the driver's license in his pocket? Doesn't make any sense."

"Wake me up when something in Homicide makes sense," one of the squad muttered.

Gonzalez finished the last of the Cheez-Its, looked out over the Pacific, and scuffed the gravel.

Ranger O'Donnell, young Coley's supervisor, approached, all starched and straight as an 8-9-10-J-Q. This man probably had a poster of Dudley Do-Right on his bedroom wall. He kept fussing with his uniform. "Rock musician, huh? They're all hopped up on coke or worse. We get drug smugglers through here. Probably some drug lord wanted to make a point." He gestured toward the entry road. "The gates were busted open this morning; they're dusting for prints now."

Gonzalez looked unconvinced. "This doesn't look like any drug hit I've ever seen. Whoever did this has a real roach in his cookie jar." He inspected the cliff edge again. "One thing's for sure—it took more than one person to rig this. We're looking for at least two, maybe even a group. Williams?"

The tech who'd gotten in trouble with his own zipper finished helping the medical examiner zip the body bag. "Sir?"

"Pay special attention to the lumber; we may learn something there." Of the rest of us, Gonzalez asked, "Some wing nuts still consider Jews 'Christ-killers.' Any of you know if this guy's Jewish?"

The M. E. cracked, "No, but when I autopsy him, I'll let you know if he's been to a *bris*."

Gonzalez politely ignored her, and popped a few Altoids into his mouth. "Why go through the trouble of crucifying someone? Gotta be a statement of some sort. But there's so many other places in San Diego that'd make a better site for a crucifixion statement. Like Soledad Mountain, for example; that'd score points. Even Sea World Tower. But here? In a nature preserve? We're missing big pieces," he rambled.

"The Preserve location reinforces my theory. You'll see—drug smugglers," Ranger O'Donnell declared. He dusted off his uniform for about the fortieth time and headed for his Jeep.

Gonzalez called after him, "I could be wrong; it's my first crucifixion!"

For the first time since I found the body, I almost smiled.

"Bernais," Gonzalez called to an experienced looking officer. "Take Ms. Camillo's statement so she can go home."

Home. Where I'd have to break the news to Lana. Damn.

5

STRANGE FRUIT

WHEN I GOT HOME, Lana and her vintage truck were gone. Why anyone chooses to drive a half-rusted piece of steel that sucks 16 miles per gallon, I don't know. She says it never gives her any trouble and has room to spare for her massage table.

I avoided Pookie and reached for Raj, burrowing my face into his neck. Raj tolerated this intimacy well, licked me a few times, then excused himself and departed through the doggie door for the backyard. Sun had conquered cloud and paradise reigned in San Diego again. Everything around me looked so normal—neighbors coming home from church or mowing lawns, kids skateboarding. I wondered if I'd ever again know what "normal" feels like.

I wandered the house. I love our home, and usually its white living room with fireplace, glass-walled sun porch, colorful kitchen, and lush backyard would cheer me up. But right now I hated anticipating the hurt Lana would feel when she returned to this home and learned about Cody. I probably cared too much. Some days I felt we were so far past the attraction that even our dogs didn't sniff each other anymore. Some days were otherwise.

When I was a kid, my favorite toys were Slinkys and Tinkertoys. Perhaps the geometric shapes—spirals and lines, hubs and triangles—engaged my mind. Whatever it was, life seemed better for having them in it. On my twenty-fifth birthday, I bought myself the Tinkertoys Classic Jumbo Builder Set. I use them the same way some people use cigarettes or rosaries, to reduce anxiety and give my hands something to do.

I got out my Tinker Toys and built something that looked like a spindly version of Notre Dame. Unfortunately, that reminded me of cathedrals, which reminded me of crosses. I grew frustrated and tired. I finally napped.

When I awoke, I played with the dogs awhile, grabbed an orange from our backyard tree, and peeled it in the breakfast nook, trying to recapture a vestige of Sunday ease. I heard Lana's key in the door. She bounded into the room. "Guess what we did in my seminar today!"

"Uh . . . plotted your astrological charts?" She shook her head No. "Applied henna tattoos to each other's chakras?"

"No! We talked to a ponytail. It was so cool." Lana was stoked; I didn't want to blow out her match so soon.

"You talked to a ponytail? Sounds hairy."

"We laid it on a chair and role-played we were someone who had just cut it off after growing it for 15 years."

My mind has difficulty with most New Age concepts. They fit Lana like a birthday suit. "Guess this wasn't a tax seminar, was it?" The silver watch was on her wrist.

"No, silly, my Expressive Arts Therapy seminar. Remember, I mentioned it a few weeks ago? Anyway, we supported this woman moving through a rite of passage about cutting her hair. See, she thought she was ugly and she cut her long hair, which everyone had said was beautiful. Then when she looked at the ponytail, she . . . ."

"You know this isn't my kinda thing," I interrupted. "Italians from Jersey don't do therapy seminars."

She laughed, "Well, anyway, it was very inspiring!" She poured herself a glass of hibiscus juice, took a long sip, and turned to me. "What've you been up to?"

I'd boiled water in the teakettle and made myself some ginger tea. I left a bag out in case she wanted some. I took a sip and fumbled for the right words.

"I drove out to Torrey Pines Preserve," I began. A Yugo for sale at a Corvette dealer would feel more confident.

"Have a good hike?" She drank the juice; scratched Pookie behind the ears.

"A man was found dead out there today." A frozen moment iced the comfort of ginger tea. I took another sip anyway and continued, "He was hanging over the side of a cliff." Deep breath. "On a cross."

"Oh, my God!" she exclaimed with no apparent sense of the irony. She looked me in the eyes. I looked away. "Talk, Tess."

Several minutes into my story, she went for the ginger tea herself. Her hands trembled as she poured the water.

When I'd finished recounting the morning's events, I didn't know what to say. I put some old blues on the stereo. Pookie snuggled down close to Lana's feet. The music helped fill the silence. Billie Holiday lamented about crows plucking strange fruit. Remembering how the ravens squawked at Cody's body on the cliff, I felt Billie had a point.

Finally Lana dried her eyes and pulled her shoulders back. "I need to do laundry. Got any lights you want washed?"

I nodded. "Thanks."

Turning back to me, she said, "I was his local fan club president for a while. I'm sure some radio station will do a tribute to him. I'll have to see how I can help." She paused, thinking. "It wasn't just his music, and it wasn't just his looks. He did tons of charity work. He cared about the environment. He was an incredibly good soul. How could anyone think he deserved to die like that?"

I wondered who thought he did.

I wondered if she'd remember to separate the whites for bleaching, but didn't want to nag her. I wondered what Thomas Paine would have thought about our current electoral process. I wondered how many IQ points we lose for each hour of reality TV we watch. I wondered if I should take a personal interest in tracking down Cody's murderers. I wondered a lot of things, then helped Lana with the laundry. Even after your own personal Calvary, you need clean underwear.

6

FINISHING TOUCHES

HIS STEP FELT LIGHT; *his breathing full and strong. He hummed to himself. He placed the coffee grinder on the workbench and plugged it in. He added a few of the teeth. ZZZSHRR! Quite a racket, but he'd expected that; enamel is hard. Gradually, the noise diminished to a low whir. He turned it off and emptied the powdery residue into the garage utility sink and rinsed it down the drain.*

He repeated this process with the next batch of teeth, moving slowly and precisely, as though he were putting finishing touches on an object of great beauty. He reached in and felt along the vehicle bed.

"Shit!" he muttered as a loose thorn pricked his finger.

He ran a portable vacuum cleaner over the same area to collect any thorns, fabric, and any other incriminating particles that might remain. He heard a clattery ping through the vacuum hose, and realized that at least one chip of tooth must have escaped earlier detection. He put the vacuum away.

He laid the new piece of carpet down on the garage floor.

He changed into his grimiest hiking boots, then stomped and wiped and kicked until the new carpet looked like something a coyote might bring back to her young. He slid the newly worn matting into the rear of the vehicle and tamped it down evenly.

He changed from the hiking boots back to his regular shoes. He unplugged the coffee grinder and took it with him into the house. There, he drew a bottle of sparkling water from his fridge, quenched his thirst, and basked in the deep satisfaction of a job well done.

7

MEEP MEEP

MONDAY MEANS WORK and work is a four-letter word ending in "k." It took me years to find a job that my head and my heart would agree on. I went to Bible college; dropped out of Bible college; sold real estate; joined the Navy; left the Navy; went back to college; changed majors from history to math; got my degree; and still floundered for a while before I felt good about earning my living. It's taken eons, but I finally found employment that offers a four-day work week, great co-workers, and economic contentment.

My employer—let's call it the Imitech Foundation, real names not being advisable—is a Special Projects subsidiary of a well-known software magnate who needs the tax write-off. (Hint: If we were a janitorial service, we would definitely do windows.) We provide customized Web software to certain nonprofits for free. Somewhere in the world, doctors caring for children in the boonies can tap into online diagnostic tools we provided. In Chicago's Woodlawn 'hood, a social services

agency trying to prevent child abuse can accept online donations via a Web site we created. And so on.

Possibly due to our unusual status, our group's work style
resembles anarchy. During our usual Monday morning staff
meeting, we cover weekend exploits, sports news, and gossip,
all spiced with sexual innuendo. Walker Boniface, our director,
squeezes in the business agenda as opportunities arise. No
pointy-haired boss, he usually allows us a little social time,
then steers us in the right direction.

That Monday morning the steering was more like steer
wrestling.

First, God had birthed the sky, spanked its butt, washed it
clean, and sent it out to play. Our office complex borders a
canyon and has large window walls through which the spring
weather ardently seduced us.

Second, everyone had heard about Cody Crowne on the
evening news; an inquisition was inevitable. Even Walker was
curious.

After thirty-seven minutes of Cody Crowne, Walker's
son's soccer exploits, the graphic designer's romantic weekend,
and overt flirtation between our admin assistant and a programmer, work regained our attention. One of our clients
wanted a mirror version of their Web site in Spanish, as well as
online transactions. We all made notes and nodded until, one
by one, we noticed the al fresco mating ritual in front of us.

Staring at his reflection in the window wall (and conse-
quently watching our staff meeting) stood a huge roadrunner
with charcoal and blue tail feathers. In his beak, he held a wrig-
gling lizard love offering. He cooed, twitching his head this
way and that, showing off his catch, doing his best to impress
the potential soul mate reflected in the window.

"Looks like Cindy's not the only one for whom the urge tolls," I quipped, with a glance at our graphic designer. She had the decency to blush.

We sat there spellbound by the roadrunner, pretending we were all mature adults who *wanted* to work this morning, but couldn't help such overwhelming distractions. Personally, I found post-murder concentration quite difficult.

Mid-afternoon, Detective Bernais called and asked me to come down to the police station to sign my statement. Never one to object to an early departure, I was gone faster than reindeer can fly.

I turned ahead onto I-5, catching a fine view of water skiers, sailboats, and volleyball players in Mission Bay Park. How can that many people not have to work at 2:45 on a Monday afternoon? Ah, California!

I took the Front Street exit, tricked my way through traffic to Broadway, and headed east. I caught a red light on Fourth and stared at the lavender, peach, and lime stucco of Horton Plaza, downtown's art deco shopping mall. The air smelled of exhaust fumes with an undercurrent of T-bone steak, from one of the restaurants in the Gaslamp District, no doubt. I made all of two blocks on the next light, amusing myself by singing along with a Catie Curtis CD. My car is like my shower: within it, I have the world's greatest singing voice. Two more lights moved me all the way to San Diego's large police station complex on Fourteenth Street.

Detective Bernais was prompt. He led me into a small room and offered coffee. I declined. My doctors believe coffee stimulates estrogen, and breast cancer feeds on estrogen. Bad enough I have a cup and a half in the morning; I don't usually risk more than that.

Bernais looked as comfortable in his black skin and his forty-plus years as any man could be. He placed a one-page typewritten sheet in front of me and I read it over. He had taken such careful notes that I didn't have to change a single word of the statement. Bright guy.

"Have you been able to make a firm identification?" I asked, signing my Jane Hancock. The morning's papers had begged the issue.

"That's official police business," he answered, then seemed to reconsider. "Not yet."

"Um, if there's anything I can do . . . I obviously have a personal involvement in this because I found the body, and I actually helped SDPD once . . ."

Bernais smiled. "I know. I read the file on your, um, previous contribution to the Belle Farby investigation." He was looking brighter by the minute. "Thank you for your offer, Ms. Camillo, but we've launched a thorough professional inquiry." He discreetly emphasized *professional*. "We'll find out who murdered Cody Crowne."

"If that's who was murdered." I looked Bernais in the eye. He looked me in the eye. He was going to toe the party line. I stood up, shook hands, and left. Maybe I should've brought him a lizard. Meep-meep.

8

TURN THE BEAT AROUND

NOTHING MORE INTERESTING than flossing happened Tuesday, so Lana and I had plenty of time to absorb every news item about Cody Crowne. Lana knew quite a bit about him, but I was learning from scratch.

The media reported that San Diego criminal forensic labs apparently had a huge work backlog; confirming identity by DNA would take months. Police were seeking relatives to positively identify the body. Cody's parents were deceased, and he was divorced. His ex-wife, Marilyn, was remarried and lived in Vista, a North County suburb of San Diego. Apparently the divorce had been bitter, because Marilyn was reluctant and uncooperative when it came to helping the police identify the body. Cody and Marilyn had no children.

Cody's one sibling, Cathy, had been born with a mild mental disability. She lived in a group home in Flagstaff.

His residence was a modest Craftsman cottage near Laguna, an art colony beach community. He didn't spend much time there, since he was usually on the road, opening for a more prominent musician. He dated occasionally but had had no long-term romantic relationships since the divorce. Acquaintances claimed he practiced Buddhism, liked to garden, did charity work, and had no apparent vices. For a one-time, bad-boy rock star, Cody sounded sinless. Of course, the last sinless guy got crucified, too.

Wednesday morning, I made us oatmeal pancakes with sliced peaches, while Lana scanned the headlines.

"Rock Star's Sister Identifies Body," Lana read loud enough that I could hear over the frying pan.

"Read on, MacDuff," I encouraged.

"'It's Cody for sure,' Cathy Crowne, the musician's sister, claimed. 'I can tell by the big scar on his knee. He got it when we were playing together.' Ms. Crowne arrived yesterday from Arizona to assist police with identification of the body." Lana put the paper down. "You think she knows what she's talking about?"

"I'd hate for my identification to depend on the Baron. He probably wouldn't remember if I had three noses." Barry "the Baron" Camillo, my brother in Jersey, was rather self-absorbed. "But it sounds like the police find Cody's sister credible."

I turned off the stove burner. "Pancakes are ready." Raj looked at me expectantly. "Sorry, dude, they're not for you." I gave him a MilkBone; he thanked me with a wag.

While breakfast was tasty, Lana seemed withdrawn and distracted. "What is it?" I asked.

"I see a lot of legs in my massage work."

"And?"

"And an awful lot of people have scars on their knees. It's hard to find someone who doesn't." When I didn't respond, she sighed. "Maybe I just don't want it to be him." She carried her plate to the dishwasher. "I'm going to hear Ismael perform at the Cafe del Morro tonight. Is your thing still on this evening?"

"Yup. I'm meeting her at Twiggs Coffeehouse at 7." My "thing" was yet another blind date through a personals Web site. Ever the optimist. It had been well over a year since my cancer surgery. I'd given myself time to heal and I was more than ready to rev my engine.

Amazing what the sex drive is responsible for—personal ads, pantyhose, perfume, perfidy. Or in this case, potential—meeting a total stranger at a coffeehouse to determine if there was any. I used personal ads because after decades in San Diego, the lesbians I knew fell into two basic categories: those who were coupled, and single platonic friends. I needed new faces. I worked with computers all day, so an online connection felt comfortable to me. Virginia's ad had caught my interest—she said she had a swimmer's body, had traveled through France, and worked in a law firm. She hadn't posted a photo, only the description, but she sounded worth a try.

Lana finished her green tea. "I'm teaching Tai Chi classes at the Rec Center most of the day, then I have a dentist appointment."

"You're going to see this hot flamenco player when you've got a mouth full of Novocaine?"

She shrugged. "He plays guitar better than he kisses." She made a silly face, and headed to her room to get ready.

I have Wednesdays off, a day to myself that I cherish. I generally spend it at the beach or in the mountains, when I can go without having to fight weekend crowds, but today would be different. I picked up the phone and dialed a number I knew by heart. I reached an automated security system and had to enter another series of digits. Finally, a familiar baritone answered.

"Roark Jurist."

"Greetings, my dearly beloved," I responded.

"Tess darling! How are you?"

"Better than most, I'm told."

I met Roark in the late 70's while dancing to "Love to Love You Baby" in Roland's, a gay bar in Portland, Maine. Which wouldn't have been notable except we were both in the navy at the time, stationed at the same base, and were trying to remain closeted.

The encounter changed our lives. Roark and I started spending time together, on and off base. We found we had much in common—a love of hot cars and disco dancing; a fascination with mathematical patterns; middle class families with middle class values who didn't understand us; and a refusal to take life too seriously.

In those days the Navy conducted witch hunts for gays and lesbians, so Roark and I decided a paper marriage would be just the thing to provide us cover. First Class Cryptographic Technician Roark Arthur Jurist and Second Class Personnelman Tessa Lynn Camillo tied the knot in a private ceremony, and went separate ways on our wedding night.

After four years, I took my honorable discharge and used my GI Bill for a non-Bible school education. Roark eventually tired of trying to make Chief, left the navy, and brought his cyber-crypto skills to an ominous and nearly omnipotent government agency, one whose real name I can't mention. One that gives congress no explanation for its budget. One that makes the NSA look like a dress rehearsal. I'll just call it Immensely Powerful Government Spooks, or IPoGS.

By the time Roark took the position at IPoGS, it was OK to be gay if you were open about it to everyone, and therefore not susceptible to blackmail. In minor, tedious ways, the marriage became cumbersome and eventually we filed for a divorce.

Phone to my ear, I turned around and disentangled Pookie from my feet. At the front door, Lana waved good-by and headed out.

My amicable ex was asking, "So what're you doing for Easter?"

"That depends; I need your help with something. Can you make like a genie and grant me three wishes?"

"You'll have to rub my lamp in all the right places."

"You guys are all alike!"

I loved his laugh. It came from deep in his chest, and never sounded phony. When its gentle rumble subsided he asked, "What do you need?"

With Roark's IPoGS connection, he had better access to information than the police. "Everything you can get on Cody Crowne."

"Aahhh."

"Practicing your deep throat techniques?"

"You *are* in a mood! Why the interest in Cody Crowne?"

"Guess you haven't been following the story closely. I found the body. Lana had a big crush on this guy, and she's afraid the police are botching the case. I want to see what's what and decide if I should jump in or back off."

"Remember what happened last time you nosed into a police matter?"

"How could I forget?"

"And you still want to do this?"

"Absolutely."

I heard his sigh of resignation. "OK, I'll get you everything I can find. Look for encrypted e-mail in a couple hours."

I made a big smooch noise into the phone. "Mucho appreciato."

"Love to love you, baby," he sang as he hung up.

That dadburn disco song played in my head all day. While I was very fond of the dance craze way back when, my musical taste has evolved. "Stayin' Alive" stayed through a lovely hike in Lopez Canyon, where I watched Painted Ladies flutter en masse. I then returned home to check on info from Roark.

After downloading everything he'd sent, I reviewed the material, printing items I might want to refer to later. Roark had sent Cody's medical and DMV records, discography, a schedule of performances for this year and last, and of course, the current police reports. I focused on the latter, but they were discouraging. All materials—the pine 2x4s, yellow nylon rope, 8″ aluminum zinc-galvanized gutter spikes, etc.—used in the murder were standard types found in every Home Depot or Lowe's, and at dozens of construction sites. No fingerprints had been recovered; the perps apparently knew enough to wear gloves. The crown of thorns on the victim's head was made from pyracantha, a plant found in many southern California gardens.

The buckwheat bushes Detective Gonzalez had been interested in yielded two gold carpet fibers, a common type used in numerous vehicles and in some indoor/outdoor carpeting. The autopsy report confirmed the time of the crucifixion as between 10:30 and midnight, most likely around 11 p.m. Police were being thorough, but they didn't have a clue. Literally.

"Rock the Boat, Don't Rock the Boat, Baby" played so

convincingly on my mental radio that I rocked my computer chair and nearly landed on my butt. I'd been reading for several hours when I realized it was time to get ready to go meet a woman with a swimmer's body. KC and the Sunshine Band played on the alpha channel of my mind as I brushed my hair and freshened my makeup. Maybe this woman would swim my alpha channel. Land on my white cliffs of Dover.

When guys say they're horny, they usually mean their testosterone level has built up and they crave sexual relief. When I'm in the mood, there's sometimes an element of physical sexual frustration, but far stronger is the longing to savor the lost-world delights of a woman's sexual nature. I love to feel pleasure rise from a woman's body and know I helped create it. I love the sounds a woman makes in utter surrender to her climax, and I love knowing a woman intimately enough to travel to that place with her. Nothing beats the experience, not even Slinkys, See's, and sinsemilla combined.

The thought of Ms. Swimmer's Body had me excited as I parked half a block from the café. An old English word for the sexual act was "swive," a *Canterbury Tales* tidbit that teachers rarely include on vocabulary lists. I longed to swive and was meeting my swimmer.

I entered the café and looked around for someone who met Virginia's description. Only two women were sitting alone—a heavy, doughy-faced Gothic with horrid posture, and an attractive Hispanic woman in her mid-20's. Criminitlies! I took a deep breath. Virginia and I had established in an e-mail exchange that we were only a few years apart in age. I headed for Gothic, but gave the chiquita a covert wink.

"Virginia?" I inquired as I approached the woman in black. "I'm Tess."

She looked at me and smiled. "You look a little like Sally Ride."

"Right." She was halfway through some concoction with a dilapidated froth. "I'll go order. You need anything?" She nixed the offer. I placed my order for decaf chai tea, using the wait to calm my disappointment.

By the time I returned to the table and began our getting-to-know-you session, I'd given myself a pep talk: don't judge by looks alone; give her a chance.

Two minutes later, I knew I could never date this woman. The remaining forty-three minutes I spent out of politeness. Her job in the law firm was bookkeeper; her trip to France was a post-miscarriage recuperation period (pregnancy courtesy of a boyfriend; bisexuality had not been mentioned in her ad). Her assessment of a "swimmer's body" must have been based on the manatee. None of that would have necessarily precluded potential, but in her every utterance she had implied or actually stated something other than the truth. I caught her in so many lies, I wanted to recommend a psychiatrist on my way out.

I told her I didn't think we had enough in common, thanked her for her time, and headed for the door. The evening air smelled of night jasmine and Chinese food from a nearby restaurant. "Turn the Beat Around" followed me all the way home, where I settled in to see what else my ex-husband had e-mailed, and to await the return of my ex-swife.

9

PLAY IT, SAM

WHEN I GOT HOME, I retrieved a second e-mail from Roark, skimmed its contents, and took Raj and Pookie for a walk. Evening offered a cool breeze; purple jacaranda blossoms formed a canopy over the sidewalk. I took my time, pondering Cody's murder as I strolled by marvelous old Craftsman and Mission-style homes.

I looped around the block, stopping to visit with my neighbor across the street, Smacker. Smacker entered the world about nineteen years ago under the name Lionel Leary, but insists on being called by his rap moniker, inspired by something to do with his kissing technique. His father, a burly black ex-Marine football coach, and his mom, a slim Caucasian grade school principal, divorced six years ago and Smacker sought refuge in rap. Wielding extraordinary personal charisma and a male model's good looks, Smacker had weathered the divorce, high school graduation, and seduction by numerous young ladies. This evening he waved from his bedroom window, flew out the front door, and hugged me.

"Tess-Lady! You got to hear my latest; it's the shit!" he informed me.

"Let it roll, Smacker," I said with a grin. He was genuinely fond of me, whether because I'm an auntie figure of sorts or due to fascination about my lifestyle, I'm not sure.

He went into full performance mode right there on the sidewalk. Break dancing a toprock, with an occasional flare or glide, he rapped the lyrics, *"I dip behind tint, keepin' condition mint / Up late night, I talk to God with a moskey, gettin' bent."*

"Um, what's a 'moskey'?" I asked.

"A moskey, a mosquito—you know." He could see that I didn't, so he offered more clues. "A mosquito; a buzz. A joint."

"Ah, now I get it. Sounds sweet, Smacker. Keep it up and I'll be watching you on Leno one of these days."

He smiled, petted the dogs, and danced back into his house. Raj, Pookie, and I were on our way back when I saw Lana's truck pull up. I hadn't expected her home until late if at all. She'd seen Ishmael the flamenco guitarist several times and seemed to like him.

By the time I got in, Lana sat in the living room in front of the TV, a fudge brownie in her hand, emitting major "I-don't-want-to-talk-about-it" body language.

"You wanna talk about it?"

She gave me a steady look. Even with my New Jersey sensibilities, I got the message.

I decide to pull in my jib and come about. "What're you watching?"

"A special, a tribute to the hundred greatest movies of all time."

"I've got an idea—let's set up your massage table and exchange back rubs while we watch it?"

Her heading shifted a few degrees toward pleasant. "Would you do me first? The Novacaine's worn off and I feel miserable."

"No problem. I'll get the table; you get the almond oil and sheets." I don't know why I insist on doing the heavy work. She's perfectly capable of carrying and setting up the massage table. She takes it to clients' homes all the time.

In a few minutes, my thumbs were pressing into tight tendons between Lana's bare neck and shoulders, stretching them, loosening them, as only someone who really knows a body can.

On the TV, Rocky Balboa ran up the steps of the Philadelphia Museum.

"How was your blind date?" she inquired.

"A once in a lifetime experience, I hope."

She chuckled. "Ooh, right there." I worked with quick little circular movements.

"I've decided to dig into the Cody Crowne case a bit; I got Roark to help me."

Lana raised her torso a few inches off the table and turned toward me. "What'd you find out?"

"Calm down," I said as I nudged her back down and worked her shoulders.

"I've only had a chance to skim the stuff, but . . . let's see: The police think the body is Cody. Not only because of the resemblance and the sister's statement, but also because Cody hasn't surfaced anywhere else."

I could feel the letdown deep in her bones. I walked over

to the other side of the massage table. Butch Cassidy told Sundance that the fall alone would kill him.

I continued, "Cody's drummer, Real Bob McCoy, claims that about halfway through Gabrielle's last set, he saw Cody walk from the backstage men's room toward the parking lot, with some guy who had his arm around Cody's shoulder. He only got a glimpse of them. The man was about six feet tall, but McCoy couldn't see his face. He doesn't remember what the guy was wearing and doesn't know which vehicle they were headed for."

"So Real Bob McCoy was the last one to see Cody alive?"

"Other than his killers, yeah, I guess so."

George C. Scott as Patton stood erect in front of a huge American flag. I put more oil on my hands and rubbed them together to warm the lubricant before touching Lana again. She asked, "What else?"

I stood at her head and pressed, in long strokes from the base of her neck, down the paraspinals, into the hip area, stretching, stretching. In the background, Charlie Chaplin spun on a factory gear. "Police are focusing in two directions—religious fanatics, and who benefits from his will. Sergeant Gonzalez thinks the killer must be a religious nut. But they did determine that Cody's not Jewish."

Lana interjected, "I could've told them that. He's practiced Buddhism for years."

"I suppose Christian fanatics might be just as resentful of Buddhism, but it doesn't tie in to a crucifixion like Judaism does. Anyway, another investigator, Sergeant Bernais, thinks the crucifixion is a smoke screen to divert attention. He wants to know who inherits what. They're waiting for Cody's lawyers to release the contents of the will, but the lawyers aren't sure the body is really Cody."

"Interesting. Can you do more on the sides of my neck?"

"Sure." I lathered up with oil again, and kneaded Lana's soft skin. "The autopsy report showed traces of duct tape across Cody's mouth. Duct tape was also used to hold a blindfold in place."

"A blindfold? Don't kidnappers usually do that if they're *not* going to kill you? So you can't identify them when they release you?"

I thought about that while an Arab waved a scimitar threateningly at Indiana Jones. Jones pulled his pistol—ka pow!

"The blindfold actually makes sense to me. Most people who are blindfolded probably think just what you did— 'They're not going to kill me; I'm going to live.' Could've been a smart strategy if there weren't a lot of them to keep Cody subdued. The other thing is, if he could see enough to guess their intentions before those nails went in him, he would've fought like a crazed animal. Maybe the blindfold was their way of keeping him compliant."

"Makes sense, in a sick way," a more relaxed Lana mumbled.

"What I don't get is why a peaceful, garden-loving Buddhist has such a bitter divorce that his ex-wife won't even help identify his body. I'm going to scrutinize the police interviews with his ex. What I know already is this: They divorced five years ago. She remarried a guy named Tim Dandurand. He works as a manager at Legoland."

"Ooh, if you go, can I come, too? I want to try the rides," Lana pleaded as Burt Lancaster locked lips with Deborah Kerr in the surf.

"We'll see. Anyway, as far as money goes, the info Roark sent said that long ago Cody decided that when he reached a yearly income of $75,000, he'd turn the rest over to charity. Some years during the 80's he'd made close to half a million; these days he was barely making the 75 grand. He was comfortable, but no millionaire." I shook my arms. "I gotta stop; my hands are starting to hurt." I'd been massaging her for 45 minutes.

"That's fine; I feel better. Give me a few minutes and I'll do you."

Having this kind of treatment available at home sometimes makes it difficult to go out on blind dates. I stripped, lay down on the table, and heard Hannibal Lecter murmur, "Memory, Agent Starling, is what I have instead of a view."

Lana put her hands on me and I soon forgot every ache and care. God, she was good, intuitively knowing exactly where and how to touch. She shared her perspective. "Maybe his ex-wife got mad because he gave away so much money. Have you noticed that greed can really warp people's energy?"

"Umm." Something in my neck popped and it felt marvelous. My muscles, nerves, tendons were melting; I was zonked. Lana kept rubbing, the TV kept humming, and I may have dozed off for a few moments.

She suggested I roll over on my back so she could do lymphatic massage on my left arm and pectoral area where some lymph nodes had been removed. That tissue loves and needs stimulation.

Forrest Gump ran an entire football field and beyond.

As I turned over, certain ideas fell into place like steel balls into the pockets of a pinball machine. I tried to think of how to put this. "Seems to me Cody had a naiveté to him, an innocent kindness that most of us lose by fourth grade. Like Forrest Gump. Or Rose Nyland of the *Golden Girls.* Chauncey of *Being There.* For that matter, maybe even Jimmy Carter."

"Don't get started on politics," Lana objected. "We have enough of that this year."

"OK, OK. Anyway, there's something appealing about a person too simplistic for the artifice of society. They call them Holy Fools. I think Cody was like that."

Lana was quiet for a while, then offered, "The highest card in Tarot is the Fool." She concluded the massage with a scalp rub.

I got down from the table, grabbed my robe, and tried to return to the real world of our living room. I felt spacey, endorphins flooding my synapses. Ingrid Bergman whispered, "Play it once, Sam, for old time's sake."

"Want to join me for our Easter egg hunt on Sunday?" Lana's Tai Chi class had decided to sponsor the event for their kids and grandkids.

Easter, I thought. Roark had asked me what I was doing for Easter. A few days away and I still didn't know. What better time to track down the crucifier of a holy fool than Holy Week?

Lana, attributing my delayed response to mental fog, said, "I'll ask you again in the morning. Good night." She folded the massage table with ease and headed to her room.

That night I dreamed that Cody wandered into my old Biblical history class, sat down beside me, and explained that at the real Last Supper, they served liver with fava beans, and a good chianti.

10

LUMPY GRAVY

ON GOOD FRIDAY I asked my boss, Walker, for a brief personal leave of absence. He approved it, and I did my best to wrap up loose ends on my current project by the time I left that evening.

Many companies had closed at three, so at five-thirty, traffic wasn't its usual abomination; I got home in time for the six o'clock news. I stir-fried tofu and veggies in tamari sauce, walking back and forth from kitchen to living room to catch the news highlights.

Boston is an issues city; its TV news leads with an exposé on war profiteering or some social injustice attacked by yet another Kennedy. Washington leads with stories about power, gaining it and losing it. Chicago is business—hog brokers and shareholders fill its headlines. LA is show biz.

But San Diego? . . . Well, barring a super media event, San Diego leads with the 79-year-old woman who communicates with space aliens by means of cricket legs glued to her microwave. Or the mosh pit with 40 fragrances of surfboard wax smeared on its walls. Or the UCSD engineering student who robotized his VW bug to pump its own gas, the video of which looked like two metallic prairie animals mating.

This would be followed by ten minutes of sports news, even when only two minutes of anything remarkable had occurred. Later in the show—if there's time—the station might squeeze in a moment of politics, international affairs, and natural disasters. The only thing that seems to compete with local color is a juicy celebrity scandal.

I ate in front of the TV and listened while seven people told reporters they'd spotted the wayward okapi in canyons, in Balboa Park, along the freeway, and in one case, in a fitness center shower stall. A zoo spokeswoman explained that although the okapi was diurnal, it was a solitary, shy animal so daytime sightings weren't likely. I told myself that daytime sightings weren't likely because the okapi had probably become a coyote's version of eatin' good in the neighborhood.

Eventually a reporter gave an update on Cody's murder: police were hard at work but had no new leads and had made no arrests. I watched a travel feature on Machu Picchu with the sound muted while I brainstormed murder-solving strategies. Soon I turned off the TV and pulled out the phone book. I dialed a number in Vista and reached an answering machine.

"Mistah Tim Dandurand?" I began, trying on a southern accent. "Ma name is Ellie Redmund. Ah'm new to Vista—just moved he-uh from Et-lan-na, and Ah'm lookin' for a church to attend on Eastuh. Ah don't know anybody out he-uh yay-et, and Ah sure don't know the churches, but Ah saw in the paper that you lived in Vista . . ." I wasn't sure which would run out first—the voice mail message capacity or the credibility of the accent.

The dilemma was solved when a man with a calm but colorless voice picked up the line. "This is Tim Dandurand. I was screening calls because there've been so many reporters, but I'm glad you called. I'm a deacon at the Church of the Living Christ here in Vista. Our usual service is at ten, but on Easter there's also a special sunrise service. Would you like to join us for that?"

In a smaller group of people, I might be conspicuous. I replied, "Ah cain't make the sunrise service, dahlin'—at ma age Ah need ma beauty sleep! But Ah'd love to go at ten. What's the ed-dress?" I wrote it down. "Why, thank ya'll so much."

"No problem. My wife Marilyn is active in the women's welcoming committee. Be sure to introduce yourself."

"Ah feel blessed already. See ya Sunday, Deacon!"

I walked around Pookie, retrieved my address book, and looked up the number for Reynold Dill in Burbank. On a freelance basis, I'd helped create lucrative, award-winning Web sites for Dill, one of the largest music producers in the industry. He knew good music, wild but discreet women, and enough dirt on people in power to usually get his way. I liked Reynold.

He answered. "Dill here."

"Reynold, it's Tess Camillo from San Diego, the woman who did the database work for your Web sites? I'm also the one who found Cody Crowne's body last Sunday." I decided to forego social niceties, and immediately remind him of how I could be helpful to him as an inside information source in a town that thrives on gossip.

"Yes, yes; you'll have to fill me in on all the details!"

"Sure, for your ears only. But first I need a favor. You're in the biz; what can you tell me about Cody's drummer, Real Bob McCoy?" Dill could get me spin about drugs, marital affairs, and so forth, the kind of information Roark's sources couldn't always provide.

Reynold's tone was interested. "He and Cody've been playing together almost twenty-five years, off and on. Funny you should ask about him. There's been some talk recently . . ."

"What kind of talk?"

"Legal trouble, I think. Tell you what—I'm having a party tomorrow night; Real Bob'll be here. Why don't you come up and join us? Get to know him yourself. Bring someone if you want. About nine? Ciao."

I'd gotten exactly what I wanted; Reynold had gotten what he wanted. That makes for a happy relationship in Tinsel Town.

I sat down to study the new information Roark had sent. There was no mention of any legal problems or lawsuits. There were, however, other interesting tidbits.

Later, I turned the TV back on and caught the end of *Law and Order*, two campaign pitches, and an ad for a blood pressure medication. I channel-surfed and got a commercial for a cooking product that prevents lumps in your gravy. I can't make a smooth gravy to save my soul, so I wrote down the 1-800 number.

The word lump takes on nuances for breast cancer survivors. I don't want lumps in my gravy; I don't want lumps in my breasts. I remember only too well how the skin around the tumor dimpled like an orange peel; how the lump seemed to grow so that I couldn't tell where lump stopped and breast began. How, for long weeks between diagnosis and surgery, Death crawled under the covers with me every night. For an invasive carcinoma, nine centimeters is one hell of a tumor.

Lana returned about 10:00 p.m., disrupting my introspection. She was aglow about a new guy she'd met in a Learning Access class. "He's so, you know, sure of himself, but not in that obnoxious way most men are. And he smells good."

"What's his name—Paco Rabanne?" I teased. As with much of my humor, Lana ignored it.

"His name's Gable. He does marketing for a feng shui school in North County. Best of all, his Mars is in Scorpio."

Lana and I exchanged looks. Astrology is a dicey subject in our household. I consider putting your faith in astrological charts on a par with reading goat entrails. Lana considers me narrow-minded for disbelieving. To keep peace, we avoid the subject. But I knew what she was telling me: my Mars is in Scorpio and it's one of the things she found attractive. "Just how good is this guy?" I inquired.

She hesitated, then answered, "I'd miss a poker game for him."

Every few months Lana and I invite a group of friends to the house to play poker, "smoke" bubble gum cigars, wager pennies, gossip, giggle, drink, and eat. Sometimes we even played cards. Our poker nights were sacrosanct informal therapy sessions that we wouldn't miss unless something momentous happened. I guess Gable was momentous. What kind of a woman would I miss a poker game for? Certainly nobody run-of-the-Milk-Duds. I diverted the conversation by inviting Lana to Reynold Dill's party. "I'd really like you to go with me, if you can."

She'd heard me talk about Dill, but she'd never met him.

The invitation proved as irresistible as I'd hoped it would; I didn't want to make the drive alone. "I'd love to go! What'll I wear? Have you seen my red shoes?"

I didn't know or honestly care where her red shoes were, but I sure wanted to know exactly where Real Bob McCoy had been at the time of the murder.

11

DEAD CHILDREN'S TOYS

ON EASTER SATURDAY, *he slowed his vehicle and pulled into the right turn lane to enter Kobey's Swap Meet at the San Diego Sports Arena. The amphitheater building reminded him of a truncated old ceramic light socket.*

He bore left and found a spot in the crowded gravel parking lot. Strapping on his backpack, he headed for the entrance.

The vendors near the gate were pros; they regularly hawked their discounted sunglasses, potted plants, silver-plated tin jewelry, scented candles, and cotton tees. A few rows back, hot car stereos and portable TVs beckoned.

The real trove lay twenty rows farther, near the rear fence. There, a few legitimate antique dealers shared space with those who spread the debris of their tenderly mangled lives onto blankets or tables, and scribbled prices on old wedding gifts, broken musical instruments, and dead children's toys. This is where he belonged.

He browsed, taking his time. He stopped at a food stand and bought a churro and coffee. He ate alone, enjoying the morning, dodging children and thickset women who hauled newfound treasure.

Eventually, he saw what he was looking for. Up ahead a dealer tried to stir interest in a collection of marvelous old Art Deco lamps. Beyond the Art Deco lamps, a young Latina minded a blanket covered with shoes, boots, and other leather goods, probably brought from Tijuana or Tecate.

He waited until a customer distracted her, then stood in the shadows and pulled the dark Frye's boots from his backpack. He placed them carefully on her blanket, wiped his fingerprints off them with a kerchief, and sidestepped the crowd in brisk retreat.

With a half-smile, he brushed the churro's sugar residue from his lips and looked up at the blue sky.

He'd tossed the hammer into a gas station Dumpster, and could have disposed of the boots that way, too. But it gave him intense pleasure to know that someone soon would carry home—maybe even wear— a pair of boots that were prime evidence in a murder case. And that person, like the good old SDPD, wouldn't have a clue.

Only one more chore to go. She knew too much, or could know too much, so he had one more annoying task to accomplish. After her, he could say as Jesus did, "It is finished." He laughed out loud at his little joke.

12

NO OYSTERS

NATURALLY, THE POLICE had asked Real Bob McCoy about his actions after he last saw Cody. According to their reports, he told them he couldn't remember exactly; that he must've hung out with the roadies until he drove home. They'd found no roadies willing to corroborate this tale.

Throughout the more than two-hour drive to Burbank, I conjured clever ways to elicit information from Real Bob and bounced my ideas off Lana. Knowing her sense of time, I also stressed that we could only stay a short while, since we had to make the drive back to San Diego tonight so I could attend Marilyn Dandurand's church in the morning.

We parked a couple of blocks from Dill's house. Dill's neighbors on both sides had Spanish mansions of stucco with red tile roofs and bougainvillea ascending the walls. Dill's home contrasted with its sleek, modern styling, like a modest Guggenheim museum. Through the security gates, I could see Eugenia, pyracantha, and oleander shrubs forming privacy barriers near the windows.

An assistant let us in, made sure we had drinks, and steered us over near Dill. He was deep in conversation with a group of four intense-looking people. All 5'3" of him was buff. His head was shaved except for a 5-inch-wide swathe in the center running from his forehead to about ten inches down his back. The broad stripe of hair was bleached blond, treated with something that made it look wet, and braided in the back. It balanced his bleached blond mustache. Somehow Dill made it all look classy.

Maybe his diminutive size allowed him to be more candid than is usually circumspect in the biz. He didn't intimidate people, so he could play it pretty straight. But play it he did; an invitation to Dill's had a thrill to it. He spotted us, and excused himself to greet us. He managed to look relaxed even when he wasn't. "Tess, glad you could make it."

"This is my friend Lana. Lana, Reynold Dill."

"Pleasure to meet you." Dill gave her a charming smile then turned back to me. "When we have time, I want to hear every detail on this Cody story; you promised! But for three years, I've been trying to get Carlos and Gloria to cut an album together. Gloria was open to the idea, but Carlos balked. Three years! Now tonight of all nights, Carlos's agent wants to talk. I can't let this slip by." He glanced back to the group of people he'd just left.

"We'll be fine. Can you introduce me to Real Bob?"

"Oh, you can't miss him. He's tall and he's got . . ." Dill's cell phone rang and he answered it. He listened and snapped it closed, and turned back toward the people he'd been talking to. One of the men was putting away his cell phone, too. Dill looked around quickly. Near us stood two older gentlemen. He took me by the elbow. "Come with me."

Lana took off in another direction.

"Tess, this is Arnold Kornblaum and his brother Jakov. During World War II, they survived eight months in Treblinka. Jakov's son Sam was my mentor." Dill dashed off to take care of business.

I'm half Italian and half Jewish—a combination that brought consternation and in some opinions eternal damnation to my grandparents' respectable households—so I felt both kinship and respect for the Kornblaums. Twenty minutes and several "konzentrationslagers" and "vernictungslagers" later, I excused myself and moved to another room to see if I could find Dill and get more particulars on Real Bob McCoy. Dill had said Real Bob was tall, but I wasn't sure what that meant to a guy 5′3″.

The main salon had two opposing walls painted black. A white wall featured a large bay window and the fourth wall was covered in fuchsia silk wallpaper. Dill sat playing a whimsical jazz piece on a white piano tucked into one corner. He had either consummated the deal or given up on it completely in the time we were separated.

Immediately in front of me, a man who looked like muscular black licorice rocked from side to side as he and Lana discussed the relative virtues of Tai Chi versus Tae Kwon Do.

I sidled to the bar and ordered Bombay Sapphire on the rocks. Only a few alcoholic beverages are worth the loss of brain cells. To me, Bombay Sapphire qualifies.

I threaded my way between groups of guests, eavesdropping while trying to look purposeful until I could talk to Dill. I learned about the Lakers' chances for the NBA championship, the enrollment deadlines for Soledad Preschool Fulfillment Center (at least two years before the child would attend), and the feasibility of investing in buffalo ranches.

I was getting an earful on whether Dr. Roper or Dr. Seidelman did the better liposuction when I caught a fragrance that sent an exquisite rush down my spine. I turned to see what earthly creature could smell like columbine, mint, and summer rain combined.

She had short black hair with a suspicious looking white streak running right through the middle. Feather eyelashes accented her violet eyes. I don't mean feather-y; I mean feather. I'd never seen anyone wear real feathers for lashes before, but San Diego can be provincial compared to Burbank.

She wore something silky and slinky and her fragrance alone was enough to put her in my fantasies for the next month. She placed her lips near my ear and whispered, "Move toward the Light."

Why is it that the women who make my heart pound can also make my mind panic? I never did get this New Age white light stuff, but in the spirit of things I decided to respond with one of my favorites. "When I cross the Bar of the Great Blue Beyonder / I know that my Maker, without pause or ponder / Will welcome my soul, For my record is scar-less / I've eaten no oysters in months that are R-less."

She smiled like autumn in Maine. "Ogden Nash?"

I shook my head no.

"Piet Hein?" she guessed again.

"Dr. Seuss."

She held out her hand. "Nova Zhenkarov. Wonderful to meet you, Dr. Seuss."

"Tess Camillo. I . . ."

"You may have misunderstood me, Tess. I work for Reynold Dill. He asked me to look for you, and when I found you, to steer you over to Real Bob McCoy. He said you were interested in meeting him."

"And 'Move toward the Light' will get me to him?"

"That's him under the chandelier." She pointed subtly. "Big red-haired fellow." She fluttered her feathers, and started to leave.

"Please—what fragrance are you wearing?"

"A custom blend," she replied with a tad of arrogance, then continued in Groucho mode, "Mobil's custom blend high octane. Glad you like it." She winked at me.

I blushed and blinked, and she was gone.

I went back to the bar for another gin. Lana had migrated to a patio and was now demonstrating some of the more aggressive Tai Chi moves to Licorice Man.

Under the chandelier a guy who looked like Eric the Red, only with less refined personal hygiene, held forth on his latest sweat lodge experience. I vaguely remembered seeing him during Cody's performance at the concert. He wore blue overalls, a black T-shirt, turquoise and silver jewelry, and moccasins. His wiry beard harbored particles I didn't want to examine, and what looked like orange Brillo sprouted from his nose and ears.

As I approached, I recognized the older man Real Bob was talking to Jakov Kornblaum. A moment later, Jakov excused himself and moved away. As he passed me I heard his aged voice mutter, "If he neets money zo batly, vhy doss he spent hiss time sveating?"

Jakov's departure distressed Real Bob, I could tell. I moved toward him. "My condolences on the loss of your, uh, on the loss of Cody."

"Thanks," he muttered. He gazed over the heads of the crowd, searching for someone apparently without success. He signaled to the bartender, and started moving in that direction. I interposed myself between him and the booze jockey. "So, I hear you saw Cody just before he disappeared?"

He finally looked at me. "Do I know you?"

"Tess Camillo from San Diego. I worked on Reynold's Web sites." We shook hands. His hand felt sticky. After the shake, I wiped mine on the side of my pants.

He mumbled something semi-polite, then picked at a scab on his forearm.

"You must have a theory on the murder?" I tried again. I knew I wasn't being my most engaging or resourceful. I was distracted. If only I'd met Real Bob before I'd met Nova.

"Cody and I were close," he slurred. "If you lost someone close, you wouldn't want to answer a million questions from people you don't even know. Nothing personal. Now, if you'll 'scuse me, I need a drink." He moved away before I could come up with a counterpoint.

Damn. Should've tried a flirtatious tact. Some guys just don't respond well to the nosy-kid-sister approach. I decided to make good use of the time anyway. I wanted to know if Nova wore a wedding ring. OK, I got off track a little; I admit it. But jeez, it'd been so very long since any woman had made me feel that way. It had been . . . since Lana.

Nova was discussing the origins of scat singing with someone who looked like a Marsalis brother. "I'm not sure whether it was Cecil Scott or Henry Red Allen who recorded that," she remarked. I got close enough to look at her hands. The only ring she wore was an intricately patterned platinum band inset with a sapphire on her right forefinger. Odds were it wasn't a wedding band. I looked around for Lana, but didn't see her. I screwed up my courage. Standing near Nova, I placed my hand gently against the small of her back.

You can tell how things are going to go in the bedroom by how a woman responds to that touch. If she moves into your hand, or moves side to side, you're in for a good ride. If she tenses or moves away, well, you'll have to make sure as Bogie once said, "The fucking you get is worth the fucking you get."

Nova moved into my hand about half an inch and gave a gentle sway of the hip. I stood there with her grooving to Dill's keyboard solo until a hand touched my shoulder. I turned: Lana. She locked eyes with me and we spoke silently for a moment. I nodded; she headed down the hall. I excused myself and followed her.

Lana and I scared off three preteens catching a WD-40 high in a powder room. Once we were alone she started in a soft voice, "Do you think you got a little distracted maybe? Don't we need to drive all the way back to San Diego tonight? And don't you want to get up for church in Vista tomorrow morning?"

She has this miserably effective non-accusatory way of asking questions to prove her point. She was right. I knew she was right. She knew I knew she was right. And she knew if she was right, I wanted wrong.

13

CLEAR-YOUR-CHI INQUISITION

I CONFESSED TO LANA my lack of success with Real Bob. It was time to go to Plan B, which required her cooperation.

"The cops have interviewed him three times already and all they get from him is a bunch of bull. I didn't get anywhere with him. You've told me yourself that your massage table is like a confessional. People tell you all kinds of things when you get them relaxed."

"Yes, but I keep it all in strictest confidence; you know that." She shook her head. "You don't want me to abandon my professional ethics, do you?"

I've known priests and psychiatrists who take the confidentiality issue less seriously than Lana. "Think about the pain Cody suffered," I urged. "Don't you want justice?"

"Yes, but . . ."

Lana shifted uneasily. I let my eyes do my pleading.

Finally she sighed, "OK, but I'll only tell you things that relate to Cody or the murder. Anything else is privileged."

"Deal." We firmed up our plan, and I returned to Dill's party. What I now relate I learned from Lana on the drive home.

She found Real Bob by the bar. "You look so tense, " she began as she touched him on the arm. "You're Real Bob Mc-Coy, aren't you? My name's Lana. I'm a massage therapist from San Diego."

He gave her a curious look. "San Diego? I was just down there. Long way to come lookin' for business, isn't it?" he asked, slurring slightly.

"I couldn't help notice your tight neck muscles."

He touched his neck. "It's been a tough week."

"There's a small patio off the dining room no one is using. If I can find a chair the right height, I can work those muscles for you. Free of charge," she clarified.

Real Bob had no doubt that Lana was coming on to him, but if he was going to get a massage, she could chase him from here to Lompoc. He followed her into the patio where she gestured toward a teak chair. He sat down and she unsheathed her tools—a seductive voice, knowing hands, and kinesthetic intuition.

Fifteen minutes later, Real Bob was Jello. Drool drizzled from his slack mouth onto his beard. His eyelids drooped. His arms fell loosely from his shoulders. Lana moved into his neck muscles with a little more force.

"Ooo, oh, God. Umm," he mumbled.

"I'm glad this is working for you. Sometimes the best way to release muscular tension is to redirect the chi away from whatever's causing it. I sense some blockage in your heart chakra. Do you think you may be blocking out Cody's murder?" Lana asked ever so soothingly.

"How can I be blocked? I just got back from a sweat lodge Thursday."

"You poor man. Imagine how these muscles would be suffering if you hadn't done the sweat! Clearing the chi is a process; maybe with a little more effort . . ."

The preteens stuck multi-pierced heads in the patio doorway, still seeking the privacy in which to achieve aerosol-induced nirvana. Lana shooed them away with a look and continued, "Why not just tell me how you feel about Cody?"

"I feel guil—really bummed—about him. I've known him forever. We . . ." Real Bob abandoned the effort.

"It'll do you good to vent."

"I feel all kinds of things—sad, shocked, pissed off, scared. I mean, who the hell would do somethin' like that? And why?" Real Bob sighed heavily. "Ya know how sometimes you fight with your family even though you love 'em?"

"Sure."

"Well, Cody and I were like brothers. We fought."

Lana nudged him forward in the chair a bit so she could reach his spine. As he bent at the waist, she rubbed her knuckles up one side of his backbone and down the other. "Serious fights?"

"He was screwin' me out of some money. I threatened to sue him, so yeah, I guess they were serious."

"Did you feel that? Your trapezius twitched! I never forget the muscle named 'trap'ezius, because so much tension gets 'trapped' there. Why don't you try some release work about the lawsuit."

"It's all beside the point right now."

"What is? The lawsuit?"

"Whatever."

Using her most hypnotic voice, Lana tried again. "Take a deep breath and hold it for me." She smoothed her fingertips over his temples. "Now let it out slowly."

He exhaled, his alcoholic fumes mingling with the patio's soft breeze.

"There's still . . . something. Were you around Cody when the violence took place? Maybe it's the karma of violence."

"Hell, no. After I saw Cody walk away with this other dude, I packed up my gear and headed to my condo in Del Mar where I stayed the night. The cops figure I drove back to my pad here in L.A. I haven't actually lied to 'em; they just haven't asked the right questions. I'd been throwin' back a few during Gabrielle's set; I didn't want to do the drive that night."

"Why not tell the police? They'd probably respect you for not wanting to drive while you were, uh, exhausted."

"If they knew I was in Del Mar, only a few miles from where he was found, they'd probably arrest me. I'd have to hire an attorney and I sure as hell don't need more bills right now."

We cruised past exits for the town of San Clemente, which always reminds me of Richard Nixon. Lana, who reminds me not at all of Nixon, turned toward me. "I didn't find out much else, nothing relevant anyway. He got so relaxed he dozed off. I tucked one of my business cards in his pocket, in case he decides he has more to say. What did you do all that time?"

While Lana was conducting her clear-your-chi inquisition, I spent most of my time in a dark corner leaning against the silk wall getting better acquainted with Nova. Our lips had played like lion cubs in a National Geographic special—teasing, touching, brushing, almost bruising, and coming back for more.

"Oh, I just mingled 'til I cornered Dill," I answered. "So Real Bob didn't give you any specifics about the lawsuit?"

"Not really."

"I was hoping you could confirm what Dill told me. It's just gossip, but according to Dill, Real Bob claims that he actually wrote five of Cody's songs. And therefore deserves the royalties. I also found out that he drives a pickup truck with a camper shell, so he could've kidnapped Cody and hidden him and the boards and nails in the truck while he drove to Torrey Pines." I passed a driver going slower than the wrinkles on a sloth's elbow. "Did you get any sense whether Real Bob was lying or telling the truth?"

"Hard to say, especially when I don't know the person, and he'd had quite a bit to drink. I did notice something interesting, though."

"What was that?"

"When Real Bob talked about money or the legal problem with Cody, his muscles tensed. But when he talked about Cody's murder, he relaxed."

I had a headache that was growing worse by the mile, so we quieted as we sped through the blackness. We passed a fog bank settling on the twin concrete hemispheres of the San Onofre power plant like a diaphanous silver teddy over draconian breasts. We zoomed through San Diego's northerly suburbs and continued south to the Washington Street exit, then turned up the hill toward home.

Raj and Pookie wagged us a greeting, and we headed toward our respective bedroom doors. I was half way in my room when Lana called to me.

"Tess?"

"Um?"

"To leave a woman you're obviously interested in so we could come home, so you could look into the murder of a man I cared about . . . that was very loving. Thank you." She kissed me on the mouth. It'd been years since I'd been on the receiving end of those lips, but we weren't rusty.

After she retreated to her room, I thought about it. She was right; it was a loving thing to do. Must've taken my altruism supplement that morning. "No good deed goes unpunished" sprang immediately to mind.

14

TEN THOUSAND ANGELS

A STENTORIAN MOCKINGBIRD woke me up at 5:23 a.m. Apologies to Harper Lee and Gregory Peck, but I wanted to strangle its nasty little throat. A fog worthy of Scottish moors engulfed the landscape. I also started my period, which perhaps explained my feral reaction to Nova's scent and the headache driving home.

I tried to go back to sleep, but the mockingbird showed no mercy. I went out to retrieve the newspaper. It hadn't yet arrived. An Easter morning from hell. I consoled myself with peanut butter Easter egg candies and Midol while coffee brewed.

I read a few e-mail updates Roark had sent me, mostly police reports. Our tax dollars were not being wasted; SDPD was rigorously interviewing, tracking, and labbing. As in most homicide investigations, they'd focused on Cody's last twenty-four hours. When that yielded nothing more exciting than attending a charity breakfast, planting new roses in his garden, reading in his hammock (witnessed by a neighbor), changing clothes, and catching a limo to San Diego for the concert, police expanded their inquiries. They interviewed his agent, manager, neighbors, even the limo driver. They reviewed his phone bills, credit card purchases, and mail. They skimmed the files on his hard drive. All roads led to Nowhere.

I did note with interest that Sergeant Kari Dixon had been brought into the investigation. Kari was the SDPD's Gay/Lesbian Community Liaison. As such, she'd become their de facto expert on hate crimes. Since Detective Gonzalez was convinced Cody's crucifixion was a religion-based hate crime, Kari was asked to interview the "usual suspects" to determine if any of them were involved.

Kari and I had dated briefly when I was on the rebound from Lana. I hadn't really been emotionally available (though I thought I was at the time), and she had two kids who required most of her time and energy. We'd reconnected about a year ago when I was involved with another murder case, but I hadn't seen her much since.

I e-mailed Roark for information on any lawsuits Real Bob had filed and the contents of Cody's will. After the comics, crossword, and an extra half-cup of coffee, I got ready for church.

By 10:20 a.m., Lana was hiding Easter eggs for the noon egg hunt; I was hiding tears at the Church of the Living Christ as we fervently sang hymn #314, "He Arose!" I didn't have to look at the hymnal; I knew all the verses by heart.

From the age of five I'd preferred to sit in Baptist pews with my ex-Catholic Grandma Camillo, rather than attend Sunday School where the main attraction was eating paste washed down with Kool Aid, while gluing pictures of baby Moses to a bulrush basket.

Imagine a small child listening to the rectitude and zeal of Robert Duvall in *The Apostle* or Billy Graham in Madison Square Garden. Fifty-two times a year. Year in and year out. For thirteen years. Grandma Camillo may have passed on, but the legacy of the hymns remains. I cry when I sing them. Maybe it's awe; maybe it's memories of a time when life was simpler and moral lines more cleanly drawn. Maybe I'm just a sap, but the imprint's there and it's powerful.

The nave of the church was modern with a raised ceiling, honey oak pews, and colorful pennants hanging along the walls. The congregation was almost exclusively white, surprising given the motley ethnic mix of San Diego County.

I tugged discreetly at my pantyhose, trying to get them to stop binding me. I felt out of sync with the joyous faces around me who did not look like they'd been awakened by obnoxious birds, crimped by cramps, or attacked by their underwear.

To my right sat an immaculately groomed gent old enough to have played checkers with Saint Paul. Across the aisle an entire pew of teenaged girls whispered and giggled, carefully covering chin zits with cupped hands.

The pastor called for us to join in hymn #311, "Ten Thousand Angels." Inspired voices sang that Jesus could have called on ten thousand angels to spare him from crucifixion, had he not wished to make his sacrifice. Never, never sing this kind of sentimental hymn on the first day of your period. I redefined "weepy." The old gent proffered a handkerchief, which I gratefully accepted.

I'd tuned out the sermon (after hearing the same message thousands of times, it was so much "Blah, blah, blah, Ginger"), so I distracted myself by mentally analyzing where the good women of the church had purchased their Easter finery. So far

Macy's and Mervyn's were in the lead, with Nordie's and Penney's tying for a weak third place. Suddenly I tuned back in.

"A week ago today right here in San Diego County a man was found crucified, leaving us stunned at the brutality of this murder," the preacher declared. "We don't know exactly why God allowed this to happen—we won't know 'til we're called up yonder! (Praise God! Hallelujah!) But maybe God allowed this tragedy to remind us how much pain His Son suffered for our redemption. As most of you know, brothers and sisters, the victim was the ex-husband of a member of our own congregation."

Eyes turned toward a slender brunette in a persimmon-colored linen suit. Obviously, Marilyn Dandurand; less obviously, Nordie's. She lowered her gaze.

The preacher continued, "From what she's told me, not to speak ill of the dead, mind you, but the victim was a man of sinful ways. If we are appalled by an ordinary sinner suffering crucifixion, just think how God must have felt seeing His pure, only begotten Son . . ."

Next to Marilyn sat a guy with possibly the most beautiful head of hair I'd ever seen on a man. Thick curls of tawny blond—clean, shiny, and natural looking—beckoned for caresses. I couldn't see his face, but from the back, he was the perfect talent for a shampoo commercial. This might be Tim Dandurand; he certainly wasn't Tim Dandruff.

When the collection plate was passed, I tossed in a five; the hymns alone were worth it.

After the service I'd intended to corner the Dandurands for questioning but my uterus had other plans; a trip to the ladies' room was mandatory. I was banging on the tampon machine when Marilyn herself walked into the rest room.

I looked embarrassed, mainly because I was. "It ate my quarter, and I really need one."

She smiled and began digging through her purse. "I'm sure I've got one in here somewhere." Up close, she had the nervous refinement of a Del Mar thoroughbred. Her manicured hand offered me a tampon in a lipstick-smudged wrapper.

"Thanks."

"No problem." She stepped into a stall. I did likewise, and busied myself putting the tampon where it could do the most good. Afterward, I joined her at the sink while we washed and primped.

"Are you Marilyn Dandurand?"

"Yes. Why?"

I caught a strong whiff of paranoia. "This is my first time here; someone mentioned you were on the Welcome Committee."

"I certainly am. Welcome to the Church of the Living Christ." She offered me her hand. "And you are?"

"Tess Camillo. I'd love to talk to you a bit when you have time."

"Easter's kind of a busy day, as you can imagine. I'm helping with the Easter egg hunt for the kids."

Who would've guessed Marilyn Dandurand and Lana Maki were kindred spirits?

She dried her hands and headed out the door with me only a footstep behind. Mr. Non-Dandruff was waiting for her.

"Tim, I'd like you to meet Tess, er, Carello? She's here for the first time. Tess, this is my husband, Tim Dandurand."

Although feature for feature he was quite handsome, he had what shrinks call a flat affect. Great hair; stillborn eyes. No flicker, no expression. "Tess Camillo," I offered, just for clarity sake, as I shook his hand.

He immediately flinched. "I pricked my finger on some roses; it got infected."

For a strong guy who stood almost six feet, he acted like a real wuss. "Try some tea tree oil; it works wonders for that kind of thing." I shared this herbal knowledge that Lana taught me.

"Thanks, I will. I'm glad you joined us to celebrate this Lord's day. Are you new in town?" His voice had less inflection than a test pattern. Weird.

"No, just trying to find the right church."

"Well, if you want to fellowship with true believers, if you've accepted Jesus as your personal savior, this is the place. If your heart knows the brutal suffering of the cross . . . if you understand that crucifixion was the ultimate sacrifice."

"Interesting what he said about Cody Crowne, wasn't it?" I turned to Marilyn, hoping for comment. "He seemed to imply that Cody had not treated you well."

She nipped the bait with considerable vigor. "Cody didn't know the Lord. When we first married, we both attended a liberal church, and he seemed like such a caring, compassionate man. But when I found Christ, Cody found Buddhism." She said the word with the same reverence you'd give to child pornography. "Did you know that you don't even have to believe in God to be a Buddhist? Well, in Second Corinthians 6:14 the Bible says, 'Be ye not unequally yoked with unbelievers.'"

"Right. Maybe he would've converted, given some time," I suggested with absolutely no conviction.

"He was on a godless path. He even refused to let us have children. Said the world was overpopulated enough. He wanted to play God."

Tim diverted the conversation. "Cody made his own choices, and his death reminds us all of how important those choices can be. We never know when God will call us. If you want to worship where the real meaning of death on the cross, nails driven deep into flesh, is . . . oh, the pastor's flagging me down; excuse me." He departed.

Truly, Tim was buzzing to a different hummer. Marilyn was looking agitated, like fire ants had just crawled up the back of her legs. Maybe she realized she'd been exuding psychological venom right in church on Easter Sunday.

"I've got to go help with the kids. I hope you'll join us again next Sunday."

"Do you and Tim have children?" I asked.

"By the time I divorced Cody and met Tim, I was forty-one. We tried fertility treatments for a while, but . . ." She shook her head. "I've really got to go now." Marilyn headed through a side door toward a playground.

Maybe she wouldn't be very long and I could ask a few more questions. I decided to browse the church library. The shelves smelled moldy and were lined with Bibles, concordances, biographies, and paperbacks. Hal Lindsey and Frank Peretti were prominently featured. The majority of books were outdated, probably donations. In some the paper was yellowed and fragile, a breath away from being torn. (Aren't we all?) On a daisy wheel display, videotapes and DVDs rang-

ing from *The Omega Code* to *The Chronicles of Narnia* awaited victorious souls. My eyes drifted to another shelf, and there
in front of me was a hardbound copy of *He Chose the Nails*
by Max Lucado. The donor's name was still written in the fly-
leaf: Tim Dandurand.

I felt like ten thousand mildew spoors were closing in on
me. Time to get the hell out of Dodge.

Spurring along I-5 with the moon roof open, I unbuttoned
uncomfortable buttons, and reflected on my fall from Fundamentalism. Jesus, in many ways, was a charismatic, mystifying
character. He told the truth candidly, sometimes with wry humor. He despised hypocrisy. He ate fish from Galilee; soaked
his toes in River Jordan mud; sneezed in Palestinian dust. He
flouted authority, broke the law, and demonstrated genius PR
skills. Only organized religion could take a man like that and
make him judgmental and stuffy.

I put an old Indigo Girls CD in the player and listened to
their comforting harmonies. The sun had cleared part of the
fog; Easter no longer looked like a sky swamp. My cramps had
subsided; I began to feel like myself again.

Like myself. Hmmm. Do I like myself? A lot of yes with
an occasional no. I like my heart and my mind more than I like
my scar-covered body. I like my spirit but don't always know
how to nurture it. Another legacy of Fundamentalism.

I changed lanes, both tarmac and karmic, and considered
the morning's events. Why hadn't the cops arrested Tim Dandurand? That strange voice and bland expression, that fanati-
cism—what more did SDPD want?

But I knew from the police reports he had an alibi. When
Cody was being killed, Tim Dandurand was deep in prayer in

front of three other witnesses at the men's Saturday night prayer meeting.

OK, then why hadn't SDPD arrested Real Bob McCoy? He had a grudge against Cody, he owned a pickup with a camper shell, and he had absolutely no alibi. So arrest him already, right?

Not exactly. If Real Bob told Lana the truth about being in Del Mar (and why would he offer such an incriminating story if it wasn't the truth?), then he was alone. And nobody could crucify Cody Crowne and hang him from the cliff alone. On second thought, maybe Real Bob did lie about being alone.

Or maybe Tim Dandurand's prayer group were in on it together. Four grown men were more than enough to pull it off. But why would an entire men's prayer group all hate one has-been musician enough to kill him?

When I returned home, I surrendered the day to carbs, naps, Midol, loose clothes, and aromatherapy. If the mockingbird ran an instant replay tomorrow morning, I'd buy a BB gun and ten-thousand pellets.

15

INTRA LATA
DA VIDA, BABY

THE MOCKINGBIRD MUST HAVE sensed my intentions, because Monday began as peacefully as Sunday had not. After some stretches, 15 minutes of subversive meditation (a.k.a., reading the comics), and a good breakfast, I felt ready to take on the world—the world of personal finance, that is. Even amateur sleuths have to pay bills.

Irrationally, I haven't worked up the nerve to pay them online. I know too much about what a hacker with your account numbers can do. Online banking for me is still in the category of "one of these days." I got out the stack of bills that accrues between paychecks; found my checkbook, a pen, and a calculator; and sat down to work. Cable TV and Internet service, check. Auto insurance, check. Water and sewer, check. Plumber we called when the hot water heater was gurgling, a big check. All I had left were the local phone bill and the gas and electric. On a whim, I actually read all of the charges.

"Raj, come over here, fellow." Raj immediately responded to the opportunity for an ear scratch or a walk. "Raj," I asked, petting him, "Why are we paying an Equal Access Recovery Charge? I mean, is that fair? Do you get charged for that in your doghouse?"

Raj assured me he didn't, nor would he ever pay anything so outlandish.

After identifying the most suspicious sounding charges on both bills, and punching an insufferable number of digits on the phone tree, I reached Customer Service at my local phone carrier. Someone named Margaret offered to help me. I pictured Dennis the Menace's female nemesis all grown up. I could almost see the ringlets.

"Margaret, I'm calling because I'm being billed an Equal Access Recovery Charge. What is that?"

Margaret countered, "Could I have your social security number, please?"

"One five three . . ." I started to give it, then realized what I was doing. "Wait, why do you need my social security number to answer a question?"

"We use the social security number to cross reference information you provided when you signed up with our service. That way, we can verify that you really are a customer."

"How about if I come in to your office tomorrow with my bill and show it to you? Then would you believe I'm a customer?"

"As long as you bring proper identification, so we know that you are, you know, really you." Margaret seemed unflappable.

I lost interest in flapping her. Time to try the gas and elec-

tric company. Ever since California's energy fiasco, their un-
derpaid customer service reps earned every nickel, dealing
with a cynical public. I hooked one and trolled him in.

"This is Terone. How may I help you?"

"Terone, Terone, Terone, how many times have I told you
I don't want you putting weird charges on my bills without
some reasonable explanation."

Terone sounded a little jarred, but landed on his feet. "You
want me to explain your charges? Is that your question?"

"Yes, Terone, I'd like you to explain just exactly what *is* this
whopping Electric Energy Rate Adjustment charge?"

"You're not paying that, Ma'am; it's a credit."

I looked at the bill carefully. Criminitlies! Damned if
Terone wasn't right. I scanned the bill for other erratic charges.
Suddenly my utility bill had never looked so simple or legiti-
mate. I thanked Terone and hung up.

I decided to try my luck with the phone company again.
After the tortuous phone tree, I reached a rep named Angela.

"Angela, I think you guys are getting a little carried away
with making up new charges. I mean, what exactly is an Equal
Access Recovery Charge and why am I paying for it?"

"Uh, no one's ever asked me about that before. Can you
hold a moment?"

Forty-five seconds later, she came back. "OK, I got my Tax
and Surcharge Reference Sheet. Which charge were you asking about?"

"Equal Access Recovery Charge."

"That's a CPU-mandated charge on the first minute of all
originating local calls to recover the cost of implanted enchilada subscriptions."

"What?! 'Implanted enchilada'?"

"Right. It says it right here. Implemented intraLATA pre-subscriptions."

"Spell that for me." She did. I was not enlightened. "Angela, do you have any translators on staff? My masters degree never covered phone bill communications."

"Um, you're paying us to provide local toll calls to people who don't use us for long distance."

"Does that make any sense to you?"

"It made sense to the Public Utilities Commission. Is there anything else I can help you with today?"

I looked at my bill. "Yeah. What's the California High Cost Fund Surcharge? Sounds like you're just putting it to me because I live in California."

Angela again consulted her tax and surcharge crib sheet. "That's a state-authorized tax paid to carriers for providing basic residential service when the cost of doing so exceeds the charges."

"In other words, when you don't make money on us, you still make money on us, because of this tax?"

"It helps us break even. It's expensive to live in California."

"Hmmm, more so with every billing cycle. How about the California Teleconnect Fund Surcharge?"

"That provides discounted service to public schools, public libraries, and county health clinics."

If I persisted, I'd soon find myself protesting miniscule surcharges earmarked to provide talking traffic lights for the blind. I thanked Angela and hung up. If humility is a virtue, it seemed Easter Monday would provoke more spiritual growth than Easter Sunday did.

I retrieved my e-mail. Roark had obtained Cody's will! I studied it like an adolescent on his first porno site. Cody left several items of sentimental value to friends and family—some wedding photos to Marilyn, childhood keepsakes to his sister, his guitar to a neighbor's teenage son. His one and only Grammy went to Real Bob McCoy. Did he do that out of guilt? Had Cody actually stolen Real Bob's songs, then felt guilty when he was successful?

When it came to the substance of his estate, Cody's will was very clear. Three quarters of his estate went to charitable organizations—the Sierra Club, Habitat for Humanity, and Project GoodFight which offered legal support to a number of beleaguered causes, like rescuing dolphins or freeing erroneously incarcerated boxing champions.

The real surprise was the final bequeathal. The remaining quarter of the estate went to "my only child, Berkeley Crowne Havrel, date of birth, May 9, 1979, last known residence, Somerville, Massachusetts."

Whoa, an unacknowledged son somewhere in the thicket. It presented interesting possibilities. I picked up the phone and dialed Kari Dixon at work.

"Detective Dixon."

"Kari, Tess Camillo."

"Hey, Girl; it's been a while. What makes you wanna reach out and touch me at this particular moment? Couldn't have anything to do with the Cody Crowne case, could it?"

I laughed but let it go quickly. "Heard you were on the case. I've got some info the police should know about, but they can't know where I got it. Any chance we can hook up some time today?"

"If you can meet me here, no problem. You got info we can use on this case, I'll make the time. How about two-thirty?"

"I'll be there."

"See ya, Girl."

I hung up, wondering why when men called me Girl it seemed condescending, but when women called me Girl, it felt like homemade cookies. I turned back toward the kitchen for a sandwich and fell to my knees. Pookie, damn her! I was untwisting myself when Lana appeared, still in her bedclothes.

"You were talking to a woman," she began.

"No 'Good morning'?"

"Good morning. You were talking to a woman. Who was it?"

"Nobody," I lied. I knew she thought it was Nova whom I hadn't yet heard from.

She let it slide and poured herself a bowl of granola and soy milk. I made a chicken sandwich and added a dill pickle. Her breakfast, my lunch.

"Do you know that every month we pay the phone company for something called implemented intraLATA pre-subscriptions?"

Lana smiled and sang, "IntraLATA da vida, baby."

"Did you see Gable last night?"

She smiled that certain smile. "Did you learn anything useful at church yesterday?"

"The Dandurands are quite the pious pair. Marilyn's bitter because Cody converted to Buddhism, which she seems to think is a cult. Also, Cody didn't want to have kids. She wanted children, so that further strained the marriage. Her new husband has a warped fascination with crucifixion. But Tim was at a prayer meeting the night of the murder, and Marilyn isn't strong enough physically to have kidnapped Cody and crucified him by herself. Probably just wasting my time with them."

"How long do prayer meetings last?"

"Um, an hour or so, I guess. Why?" Odd question for someone as schedule-impaired as Lana.

"When did it start?"

I got up, found the police reports Roark had sent, and skimmed them for the answer.

"He told the police the prayer meeting started at 8 p.m. and lasted until around 9:15. The other three attendees confirmed that."

Lana crunched her granola thoughtfully. "And Cody was murdered some time around eleven?"

"Right."

"Well, it would be hard, but it's possible to drive from Vista to the Embarcadero in that amount of time."

I flipped back through the police report. "The cops never asked what he did afterward." I was stunned.

My guess was the police had wanted to get away from Tim Dandurand as fast as possible. Maybe he told them more than they wanted to know about Jesus. Maybe they never considered arresting an entire prayer group. Maybe Tim and Marilyn murdered Cody after the prayer meeting. Maybe a meteor really did decimate the dinosaurs.

Lana cleared her dishes and gave Pookie a doggie treat. Raj looked at me and I pulled some sliced roast beef from the fridge.

"You gave me some good advice about those utility bills, Raj," I commented as I fed him a few slices. "Couldn't have done it without you." Raj was on dog cloud number eight and a half. I turned to Lana. "What're you up to today?"

"Don't you remember? I'm teaching my therapeutic herb class at four, out in the sun porch."

"That's right, sure. Well, I'm off to visit Kari Dixon down at the station to talk about the case. Guess I'll see you later."

"See ya."

I brushed my teeth, fixed my hair, and put on an outfit that brings compliments.

Lana was still at the brunch table, sipping green tea when I opened the front door to leave. I turned back to her. "Hey, I think I know what you meant about Gable smelling good. And, uh, I'm really glad you met him." From those quarters in my heart where I'm capable of deep platonic love for her, I meant it.

I was about to put my key in the ignition when it occurred to me how many social security numbers the phone company's Margaret must have acquired by now. With telephone numbers (including unlisted ones), social security numbers, names, and addresses, how hard would it be for her to obtain credit card numbers? Margaret always was the brainy one in the comic strip.

IntraLATA da vida, baby.

16

WHY'S WOMAN

"TESS CAMILLO?" ASKED a stocky fellow in uniform.

I offered my driver's license as ID. "Yes, I'm here to see . . ."

"Detective Dixon asked me to bring you on back when you got here. Follow me." The officer waddled down one hall, turned a corner, and shambled down another. "She's interviewing someone right now; you can wait in here." He led me into a small room where I sat on a chair made of salmon pink molded plastic. Through a one-way window I could see and hear Kari conversing with an intriguing individual.

The man, probably in his late fifties, had military posture, thinning black hair, celebrity skin tone, and Pacific blue eyes. He wore a white shirt, jeans, and a leather jacket worth more than my biweekly take-home pay. He played with his black mustache as he spoke. ". . . . as Buckminster Fuller said, 'Whether it is to be utopia or oblivion will be a touch and go relay race.'" That was his prediction for mankind if we fail to apply intelligence and logic to our sociological condition. No nation can continue as we have and survive. Someday the majority of Americans will see that."

Kari jumped in. "Tell you what I see—I see how you're the most intelligent and logical scumbag been through here today. You're a convicted murderer; you're on parole, and unless you . . ."

"Death isn't the worst thing we face, you know. 'Of all the wonders I yet have heard, it seems to me most strange that men should fear, seeing that Death, a necessary end, will come when it will come.' Shakespeare knew there are worse things than dying."

"Yeah, well, I prefer to get my Shakespeare from the theater, not from felons. Now answer my question." Kari was simmering.

He leaned toward her, exuding what most women would find almost irresistible charisma. "Doesn't it ever get to you? Truthfully? I mean, you're out shopping, maybe standing in line at the grocery store and what do you hear? Vietnamese, Spanish, Tagalog, Farsi. Do you want your kids to think English is only secondary . . ."

Kari smacked her hand on the table. "I'm not here for your amusement! I asked you a question. Where were you between the hours of nine p.m. and midnight the night Cody Crowne was murdered?"

The man turned in his chair and looked directly at me through the one-way window. His gaze was fiercely intelligent, yet somehow playful. "Who's visiting today? Attorneys from the ACLU? Cody Crowne's not-so-loving ex-wife?"

"My patience is G-O-N-E-gone. Spend the night in jail." Kari rose and headed for the door.

"I attended a fundraising dinner with some like-minded people up in Temecula, then drove home. I left Temecula around nine-fifteen or nine-thirty. I got stopped by the Highway Patrol as I was coming down 805 near Balboa Avenue. The patrolman detained me for quite a while. I didn't get home till well after eleven."

Kari sat back down and asked, "You got stopped by the CHP? Why?"

"The officer said I was weaving over the lane lines. He thought I was intoxicated." The man sniffed as if the officer had the mental alacrity of the Missing Link to have even considered such a thing.

"Uh huh. So you were driving under the influence?"

"Of course not. That would be despicable."

Kari rolled her eyes and continued, "Then why were you weaving on the freeway?"

"As I explained to the officer, I was exhausted." He shrugged. "Maybe I started to doze off. He made me do all those walk-a-straight-line and finger-to-nose idiocies." The man demonstrated the latter, bringing an index finger with a crested school ring to the tip of his well-formed nose. "When he realized I was just tired, he poured me coffee from his own thermos. To help me stay awake. He followed me a couple miles, too, just to make sure."

Kari slid a sheet of paper across the table toward the man. "Write down your statement for the night in question. Include the names and phone numbers of the people you had dinner with in Temecula. We're gonna check out your story."

He practically twinkled at her. "Please do so. Once again, it's been a pleasure, Kari."

"Detective Dixon to you." Kari slammed the door, and walked in to greet me. "Hey, Girl!"

I gave her a hug. "Who *is* that? He looks too smart to be a criminal."

"Lucas Zealeaux."

I scanned my brain RAM. "He was in politics, right? Quite a while ago. Then they found out he was a neo-Nazi or something?"

"More or less. Immigrants are his hate button. His "Not One More!" campaign made a big impression on the politicos during the Reagan era. He ran for state senate; planted the seeds for what eventually became Prop 187. Might've been elected governor someday if he hadn't pulled that Cougar Leap Canyon shit."

There are events permanently embedded in the memories of San Diegans, hard as we may try to forget. The shooting spree at the San Ysidro McDonald's. The wreck of PSA Flight 182. Thirty-nine dead cult members awaiting the Starship Enterprise. The Santana school shootings. Cougar Leap Canyon.

In his enthusiasm for suppressing "illegal immigration," Zealeaux had made a vigilante "citizen's arrest" of a van full of undocumented workers as it passed through an arid canyon near Jacumba. He asked the driver to step out and show license and registration. As he did so, Zealeaux opened the van's rear doors revealing nineteen "illegal immigrants" crammed into the small space.

Figuring they were busted anyway, they started to exit the hot vehicle. But Zealeaux padlocked all of the van's doors to keep them in there. It was mid-afternoon on an August day. While waiting for the Border Patrol Zealeaux had summoned, nineteen people roasted to death.

When prosecuted, Zealeaux claimed that he *had* to secure the van doors; otherwise the immigrants would have taken off into the canyons and his "evidence" would have been lost.

The jury was more moved by the driver who testified Zealeaux refused to let him turn on the air conditioning, and held him at gun point for nearly two hours while they listened to the pleas and screams of the dying. Zealeaux was convicted of second-degree murder and sentenced to some real time.

"How long's he been out of prison?" I asked Kari.

"Almost a year. Probably didn't have a damn thing to do with the Cody Crowne case, but I call him in for questioning every chance I get."

"Why?"

"Because I can." Kari got up and stretched. She was in better shape than I remembered. "I pulled in Ned Sowkopf for questioning, too; had better luck with him."

"The guy who set fire to the Plug Nipple?" The gay bar had been torched the week of Pride Parade last summer.

"Yup. He hates us family types something fierce. And he admits he hated Cody; figured Cody was gay because he lived in Laguna Beach."

"That's a major leap of logic. Is Sowkopf in custody?"

She shook her head no. "He says he had gall bladder surgery three weeks ago; even showed me his scar. I thought for a minute it was the second coming of LBJ." Kari chuckled. "But Sowkopf's on medical disability. No way could he have done any kidnapping or crucifying."

"So why is that better luck?" I asked.

"Because I bothered to call the doctor whose name was on his disability form. The doctor—if he exists—has an office down in TJ and hasn't returned my calls."

"A non-existent Tijuana doctor? Sowkopf sounds like a damned good suspect."

Kari shrugged. "I know Sergeant Gonzalez thinks it's a hate crime, and I'll do my part. But to me, the profile's all wrong."

"How do you mean?"

"Hate perps, for the most part, have low self-esteem. That's why they need to put someone down; makes 'em feel better about themselves. And their crimes are mostly spontaneous. They see something or someone; it pushes a button that fills them with hate, then they do something crazy. But this crucifixion thing, Girl . . . someone had to really think, work out the details. Someone had the confidence to take the risks. If it's a hate crime, it's about a more personal hate." Kari sighed and seemed to shift gears.

I shifted with her. "How are your kids doing?"

She lightened immediately. I noticed her eyes were the color of my mother's old mink stole. "Simone's in fifth grade already; she's doing great. Hunter's at that 'Look, Mom, I'm Spiderman' stage. I never see him without a costume on. In our community, that makes me wonder!" I marveled how she retained such humanity in her line of work. Her expression altered and she asked, "You still living with Lana?"

I admitted my continuing domicile situation.

"Gotta be hard, living under the same roof with that much temptation!" I didn't respond and Kari dropped it. "So, what's this juicy tidbit you wanna share with us police bozos?"

"Hey, I never said that. I know better. You guys are workin' your butts off on this case. I just got lucky on a couple of things. First, Real Bob McCoy didn't drive back to LA the night of the murder. He spent the night in his Del Mar condo. And he was threatening Cody with a lawsuit."

"That'll turn up the heat on him. We had some hints about the lawsuit but weren't able to verify anything. Thanks."

"There's more. Have your team check what Tim Dandurand did *after* his prayer meeting."

Kari and I exchanged looks, which told me she understood the police had not pursued the issue properly.

I continued. "And something else. I found out what's in Cody's will."

Her eyebrows rose appreciatively. "Ka ching, ka ching! Tell me more."

"Three quarters of the estate goes to charity, but the interesting part is, Cody left the rest to his kid. He had a son, apparently not with Marilyn. Berkeley Crowne Havrel. I've got a date of birth and last residence."

Kari took the piece of paper where I'd written the pertinent information. "This could really help, Tess. Cody's lawyers might take another month before disclosing the contents of the will to us. The DA's still trying to convince them that the body is Cody."

"It's Cody, all right, but still, none of it makes sense. If you're not covering up identity, why amputate the fingertips? Why destroy teeth?"

"Why beat Matthew Shepherd to death? Why burn crosses on people's lawns? Why throw bombs into churches? Why fly jets into buildings? 'Why' is not a great question in my line of work."

"Why did the lesbian want to be reincarnated as a whale?"

"It's against my better judgement, but, why?"

"So she'd have an immense tongue and could breathe through the top of her head!"

Kari's smile stayed with me on the drive home.

17

HERBS

THE HOUSE WAS REDOLENT with sage, lavender, thyme, fennel, and other delicately greening wonders. As quietly as I could, I brewed myself some green tea.

Lana's herb workshop must have been winding down because I could hear the post-lecture question and answer session.

"So while some people have very good results with valerian, it's not for everyone. If you haven't had luck with chamomile or kava, you can try a small dose and see if valerian works for you. One more question."

A heavyset woman in a purple sweat suit raised her hand. Lana nodded.

"What kind of herb would attract an okapi?"

Never directly answering the question, a smiling Lana took the woman on a sojourn. Why do you want the okapi to come near you? How would it make your life better? Should any human interfere with the okapi's chosen path?

While Lana safeguarded the independence of outlaw okapis,

a short Filipino woman in her 60's carrying a shopping bag drifted into the kitchen and asked about bathroom facilities. I pointed her in the right direction.

She returned a few minutes later, heading for me and the kitchen instead of Lana and the sunporch. She reached into her bag and pulled out a baking dish covered with aluminum foil.

Inclining her head in the direction of the sunporch where Lana was hugging farewells she said, "She's so sweet to share her time with us; I wanted to thank her with this." She spoke in a soft voice as though it was our little secret.

I peeked under the foil. What I saw looked like egg rolls. "What is it?"

"Lumpia. Tell Lana it's lumpia from Lily."

Must be National Alliteration Day. I thanked her, put the dish in the fridge, and walked her to the front door.

When the workshop guests had departed, I went back to find Lana. Unaware of Lily's gift, she was in the kitchen fixing tabbouli and hummus.

"Everything go OK?" I asked.

"Every time I teach one of these classes, I remember how good it feels. I love working with herbs," she effused.

I envied her enthusiasm. I shared with her what I'd learned from Kari about Lucas Zealeaux and Ned Sowkopf. Thinking about the warped possibilities of men like that had drained me. I really wanted mocha almond ice cream.

Lana must have sensed something. She touched my shoulder. "What's wrong?"

"Cody's killers are getting away with murder. Neither the cops nor I have any idea who drove spikes into his wrists— pulled his teeth without Novocaine—hacked off his finger-tips." I rolled my head to loosen my neck muscles. "In the past few days, I've learned that Real Bob McCoy may or may not have filed a lawsuit that may or may not have something to do with why Cody was murdered. I learned the Dandurands are borderline fanatics. I learned Cody had an illegitimate son and that Kari's hate crime work involves some real assholes. What I *didn't* learn is who killed Cody."

Lana poured her voice like melted butter. "Tess, I appreciate your trying to help. But there's only so much you can do. Don't be so hard on yourself." She dabbed hummus on pita and took a bite. She was drinking tea, but there were so many fragrances lingering in the air, I couldn't tell what kind.

"I've got an idea," she announced. "Let's smoke. We haven't done that in a while, and maybe it'll give us a whole different perspective on the facts." Lana is good with all kinds of herbs —legal and otherwise.

"Why not? It's either that or mocha almond ice cream."

Lana got her bong, we lit a match, and soon the hornet's nest of Cody Crowne's murder seemed both closer than before, and at the same time, very small, very distant. As Lana said, a different perspective.

For the next forty minutes, we did something we never did when we weren't stoned—we reminisced about the times we shared romantically and sexually, times that are normally too taboo for us to recall: the night we spent at the Hotel Del; the picnic on a warm October afternoon followed by al fresco lovemaking; the train trip up the coast. I was glad we could now cruise that memory lane without a crash helmet.

Eventually, as children do to their parents at the most inopportune moments, Raj and Pookie demanded our attention. It was Walk Time. Lana looked at me. I looked at her.

"I can't go," she giggled. "I'm too zonked. I couldn't handle anything weird that might come up. You take them, Tess. Please?"

That's how a dachshund of diminished mental capacity, a debonair Welsh terrier, two leashes, and I (in an altered state of consciousness) happened to be out walking through the neighborhood. Twilight flickered. Natal plum bushes coaxed their crimson fruit out from thick green leaves. Yellow jackets busily constructed paper nests under a neighbor's garage eaves. Spring evenings percolate potential.

Soon I was able to think about other things besides murder. My heart felt lighter; even the dogs seemed to step livelier. I wondered if Nova liked dogs. Yes, I decided; she'd like dogs. I wondered what her feathered eyes were watching right now.

Suddenly, I caught something out of the corner of my own eye. A blur of movement, maybe a headlight. With a sensation like someone blowing breath on my neck, I felt I was being followed. I pulled Pookie and Raj closer. A low, protective growl rose in Raj's throat. I looked behind me but noticed nothing unusual.

On rare occasions, I can get a little paranoid when I'm stoned. That must be what it was, I assured myself—a simple case of stoner paranoia. Suddenly, out of nowhere, I felt a hand on my shoulder. I jumped!

"Tess, it's me, Smacker. You OK?"

I relaxed. "Got buzzed by a moskey; now I'm seeing things in the shadows."

Smacker laughed. "I know that one. Hey, I wanted to tell you, my new band—the Sick Xhibit—we're layin' down tracks this coming Saturday! We saved enough to rent the studio for four hours!"

"You're going to do great things, my man! I want to hear those cuts when they're finished." I punched him in the arm, then headed off toward my house.

That night I lay in bed and listened to baby possums and their mamma climbing the oleander branches behind my bedroom window. The fragrance of eucalyptus blew in on the breeze; moonlight danced the Charleston on my floor. Sensuous images of both Lana and Nova flooded my imagination, and I touched myself. Many caresses later, my hips pressed upward in a multi-textured orgasm.

It had been a long dry spell for me, but dry spells are what make the other spells so . . . spellbinding. Cody may be dead but I was alive, and I needed to spend tonight just living. Not investigating, not analyzing, not working.

Just living.

18

SLICE

AS HE DROPPED HIS FARE *in the coin till, he tried to remember how many years it had been since he'd taken a bus. He'd ridden the Tijuana Trolley and the Coaster Train occasionally, but no buses.*

Inner city transportation had improved. The bus interior was clean and the passengers looked approachable, even at 9:00 p.m. In his blue twill slacks, white cotton shirt, and nondescript shoes, he looked like any other workaday guy whose wife used the only car they could afford. There was nothing memorable about him, which is exactly the way he wanted it. He pulled his ball cap down a bit and made eye contact with no one.

To distract himself, he read the advertisements posted inside the bus. He noticed one for the soft drink Slice and uttered a soft growl at the irony. He didn't like what he was about to do, but the police might eventually get around to asking the right questions, and if they did, she could mar the beautifully crafted masterpiece it had taken him so long to design.

He crossed and uncrossed his legs. Nervous energy coursed

through him, but he contained himself, aware that the blade strapped to his ankle could poke if he wasn't careful.

When he reached the stop, he practically leapt from the bus into the night air. Noise from the freeway buzzed in his ears. He adjusted his backpack and walked the few blocks. Her house was easy to find. Making sure he wasn't observed, he approached her front door and knocked.

That precise moment when the knife severed her flesh, he felt astoundingly alive. Adrenaline transported him into a keen fight-or-flight mode. The ease with which the blade traveled surprised him; he'd expected it would take more effort. Before he knew it, the blade hit something hard, probably a cervical vertebra. He released and she sank to the floor. She'd have no stories to tell the police—or anyone else for that matter.

Calmly, he rinsed the knife in her kitchen sink. In her bathroom, he showered and changed into the clothes he'd brought in the backpack, then stuffed the bland but bloodied clothes back into it. After he retrieved his vehicle, he'd dispose of the backpack in a Dumpster in Lemon Grove, far from here and far from his home.

He placed the Bible exactly the way he wanted it and wiped his fingerprints from everything he'd touched. Donning gloves, he let himself out the back door, closing the locked door behind him.

Now she could rest in peace. And he could sleep peacefully.

19

ANYTHING JUICY

THE NEXT DAY I AWOKE with my chi in overdrive; the break had done me good. After breakfast I took a glass of iced ginger tea out to the sun porch to do some serious criminal profiling. Lana drifted between reading the newspaper, polishing plant leaves, and trying to find Pookie's leash. I suspected her buzz from last night hadn't quite worn off.

"What do we really know about the killer?" I asked myself, ready to scratch answers on a notepad.

"What? I'm on the phone," Lana responded from the doorway between the kitchen and the sunporch, apparently having added another activity to her wanderings.

"Sorry," I mouthed.

"My dentist's office; trying to get an appointment for the permanent crown." I heard her make some "uh huh, OK" noises, then the phone receiver clicked. She called to me; "They have to see if he can squeeze me in before his vacation. They'll call back."

I'd drawn two columns on the notepad and had come up with this:

Certain	Probable
Knows San Diego area (knew no guards at the Preserve at night)	Owns truck or van
Familiar with New Testament (knew about crown of thorns)	Physically strong; probably at least one male involved
Was at Embarcadero by 10:15 or 10:30 the night Cody was killed	Knew Cody?
Had access to vehicle where things could be hidden	Wanted to make identifying the corpse difficult?

"Take a look at this and see if I'm forgetting anything," I called into the kitchen where I could hear her opening and closing cabinet doors.

"That's strange," she remarked, entering the sun porch. "I've looked everywhere. You walked them last night—where did you put Pookie's leash when you got back?"

"I certainly didn't hide it with the tuna and Total. I hung both leashes by the door where we always keep them. Raj's leash is still there." I was too preoccupied to care much about dog leashes. "Here, read this and see if I've overlooked anything."

Lana took the notepad and looked it over. When her inscrutable eyes returned to mine, she wore an odd, sad smile. "You overlooked the obvious, Tess. We know, for certain, that the murderer is capable of real evil."

"Isn't 'evil' implied with murder?"

"No, no. I mean this wasn't a crime of passion and somebody didn't just get rough after too many beers. It took a dark soul to plan Cody's murder; to abuse and torture him; to use poor Cody to send some strange message. Under *Certain*, you should include evil."

I was coming from head; Lana was coming from heart. Lana would say it was my Mercury in Virgo and her Sun in Pisces. Sparing me astrological guidance, the phone rang. Lana picked up, expecting the dentist's office, then handed it to me with a look that said don't tie up the line.

"This is Tess," I answered in my most seductive voice, hoping it was Nova.

"Hey, Girl, it's me," Kari began. "Thought you'd want to know—we located young Mr. Berkeley Havrel."

"Let me guess—in Berkeley?"

"At a rave in Boston. Bernais and Gonzalez are working with the police out there to question him thoroughly."

"Is he a suspect?"

"Too soon to say. I also confirmed that Lucas Zealeaux was detained by the CHP the night of the murder. In fact, I know the officer who stopped him, John Barkovic."

"How do you know a CHiP?"

"Everyone knows John—he speaks at a lot of civic events. Guy's a 24/7 Eagle Scout. He went to Valorum Academy, for chrissake."

"That's up there with the Citadel for upright and uptight."

"Yup. He remembered pulling Zealeaux over. Zealeaux's alibi is solid."

"What about the other guy, what's his name, Sowkopf?"

"We finally heard from Ned Sowkopf's surgeon. He verified the gall bladder surgery. Said if Sowkopf crucified anyone, he had a hell of a lot of help. Sowkopf's a loner, so chances are slim."

"This isn't the most uplifting news. You got anything juicy?"

"Oh, I got plenty of juicy, Girl, but you're talkin' professional, right?"

She caught me off guard with her flirtation and I laughed. "Professional juice for now; later, who knows?"

"Tim Dandurand has no alibi for after the prayer meeting. Claims he drove around for a while then went home. Wife said she was already in bed watching TV when he came in and she didn't notice the time. How's that?"

"Promising; very promising."

"You know what they say about alibis—the innocent don't know they're gonna need one."

"Maybe. Anything else?"

"As a matter of fact, yes. Real Bob McCoy has disappeared."

"What do you mean 'disappeared'?"

"He's gone. Like Amelia Earhart. Judge Crater. Jimmy Hoffa."

"Jesus!"

"Last seen rising up in a cloud; not seen since. Yeah, I guess he fits," Kari joked. "We've got an APB out on McCoy. May mean something; may mean nothing, but sure smells funny."

"I can't tie up the home phone line much longer; Lana's waiting for a call. Can I call you back on my cell?"

After a few seconds of strained silence, Kari answered, her

tone all business. "No need; we're done. Give me a call if you learn anything I should know about."

"Will do. Thanks." I heard the click of her receiver while I was still speaking. Jealousy is a green meanie.

20

BIDETS IN HEAVEN

I CLICKED OFF THE PHONE, placing it in front of Lana who was now checking Pookie's ears for mites, and headed to the bathroom.

The doorbell rang. It never fails. FedEx arrives with your package right when you are in the midst of what Miss Marple might delicately term a daily constitutional. The long-awaited phone call from a love interest rings as soon as the shampoo is lathered. God has decided there's something amusing about our human need for bathrooms and frequently uses it for comic relief. Don't count on bidets in heaven, but if you find them, expect to be paged by Gabriel as soon as you're positioned.

I re-entered the living room where I discovered a confused Lana dealing with a man and a woman, both in full SDPD regalia. All heads turned toward me.

Lana quickly spoke up. "Tess, these officers need to ask us some questions."

Her eyes met mine and I knew we were both thinking about the magic dragon that we puffed last night. Could the smell have traveled to a neighbor's? What was the penalty for possession of less than one ounce of marijuana these days? I tried to relax. No sense acting guilty; Lana was doing enough of that for both of us.

I offered my hand to the woman. "I'm Tess Camillo, Lana's housemate. What's up?"

"I'm Officer Tenjack; this is Officer Lopez. We just need to ask a few questions." Tenjack had red hair, the coloring to go with it, and enough extra weight to make chasing perps on foot a challenge. I liked her immediately. Lopez struck me as cagey. He was scrutinizing our living room.

"Ms. Maki was just telling us that she was home with you last night." Officer Tenjack managed to make it more a question than a statement.

"Yes, we were both home last night. What's this about?" I asked.

Tenjack and Lopez exchanged a look and Lopez inquired, "Ms. Maki, do you know a woman named Lily Cabigao?"

Lana seemed even more confused than before. "Uh, yes."

"How do you know her?" he pursued.

"I met Lily about six months ago when I did massages at Sharp Hospital. She's a widow; she works in the gift shop there. She's a good gardener. She gave me tips on how to grow herbs and flowers."

"Have you ever been to her home; do you know where she lives?"

"Yes; she invited me over to see her garden once. She lives in the Clairemont area, right off 805, if I remember right. Is she OK?"

Officer Tenjack took over. "Mrs. Cabigao was found murdered in her home this morning. Her throat was cut." She gave us a moment to catch our breath. "Your phone number was written on her calendar for yesterday. We're wondering about the connection."

"Oh, God; poor Lily!" Lana sank into the sofa, moist-eyed and stunned.

Lopez waited a few seconds, then asked again. "Ms. Maki, why did she have your number on her calendar yesterday?"

Lana struggled to control the quiver in her voice. "I'm a certified herbalist; I gave a workshop on therapeutic herbs yesterday. Lily attended."

Officer Lopez practically pounced. "I thought you were a massage therapist."

"I'm a licensed massage therapist, an herbalist, and a Tai Chi instructor. I do all three," Lana responded.

"She's also a human being with feelings," I interjected.

Tenjack gave Lopez a "cool your jets" glare.

"Was it a robbery?" I wanted to know.

Tenjack replied, "We're not sure," then asked Lana, "What time did Mrs. Cabigao attend your workshop?"

"Four o'clock."

"And there were other attendees?"

"Sure; eight people came. In numerology, nine is the number of spiritual perfection, and when you add in me as the instructor . . ."

Officer Tenjack interrupted. "Did you notice anything unusual about Mrs. Cabigao? Did she seem afraid in any way?"

"No, not at all. She seemed perfectly normal." Lana looked toward me. "I can hardly believe she's . . . ." She choked up again.

"Did she mention any plans for the evening? Perhaps mention the name of someone she was going to see last night?"

Lana shook her head. "No. We were more acquaintances than close friends. Sorry."

"Do you know if Mrs. Cabigao held any strong religious beliefs?" Lopez wanted to know.

Lana shrugged her shoulders. "She was Filipino; she was probably Catholic. Why?"

"Some printed religious material was found next to her body," he answered evasively.

Lana and I looked at each other in bewilderment. Finally Officer Tenjack spoke up. "Ms. Maki, could we get the names of the people who attended your workshop? Perhaps Mrs. Cabigao mentioned something to one of them."

Lana jotted them down for her. "Anything else?"

"How about one of your business cards? I love a good massage," Officer Lopez said with enough sleaze to grease a griddle.

One look at Lana told me she wanted nothing to do with this guy. I walked over and put my arm around her waist. "Sorry, Officer, she doesn't do men."

He nodded knowingly and both Tenjack and Lopez departed.

"Thanks," Lana said.

"You OK?" I was pretty shaken up myself, remembering the little lumpia lady.

"I guess. Just lots of emotions. First I thought they were going to arrest us for the pot. And then I learn a sweet soul like Lily has been murdered. I need to process all this." Lana sniffled as she walked back toward her room.

Her processing must have worked, because an hour or so later she ambled back out to the sunporch where I was still

Sherlock Holmes-ing. She held up Pookie's leash triumphantly. I raised my eyebrow.

"I remembered! When I was polishing one of the plants in the dining room this morning, I thought the leaf polish might be good for the leash's leather, so I polished it and left it in there to dry."

There are times Lana comes up with statements to which I can think of absolutely no response. Leaf polish as leash polish was one of them.

A few minutes later, the dentist office called back. I overheard Lana confirming, "The twelfth at 10:00 a.m. No solid foods for at least three hours afterwards; I'll only be able to sip beverages or soups. Got it." For about the hundredth time in my life, I wondered what inspires some people to become dentists—to spend their lives with their hands in people's wet mouths, scaring the crap out of most non-dentists, while bearing the onus of not being "real" doctors. If I were going into patient care and didn't want to be a physician, I'd opt for optometrist, pun intended. People would be grateful that I helped them see, and no one would associate me with drool and drills.

After she'd scheduled her appointment, Lana took a long swallow of water and announced, "I need to create some positive vibes. I think I'll take the kids to Dog Beach."

Dog Beach is a block of oceanfront heaven for canines. Located in the freeze-dried-in-tie-dyed neighborhood of Ocean Beach, all of its sand and surf are dedicated to dogs. Labs try out for the minor leagues; poodles fulfill social engagements; schipperkees sniff at kelp; shepherds play Frisbee; border collies chase skittering crabs; owners just envy the dogs.

"I want to go!"

"Aren't you immersed in detective work today?"

My inner child was yanked back to outer adulthood. "Right. See you when you get back."

I studied my notes again. I vaguely remember hearing Lana and the dogs go out the front door. "Make identifying the corpse difficult" just didn't fit. Yes, the fingertips and teeth were removed. But the killer didn't hide Cody's identity; he even left Cody's wallet. Why else remove fingertips and teeth?

I got out my Tinker Toys and built, keeping hands busy and letting mind wander. Somewhere on my mental horizon, an idea was trying to flag me down. Something someone had said or done had set a conceptual tsunami in motion, but at this point it remained far below the surface. Something about cops? Dentists? Dogs? Like the word that won't come to you when you want it, the harder I tried, the more elusive it was.

I recalled Lana's observation—this killer is evil. I added Kari's theory—hate, but personal hate. Personal. Knew Cody. Knows San Diego. Knows the New Testament. Could've been at the Embarcadero that night. Physically strong.

One suspect fit the profile almost too well, but I had to know more. I had to know what kind of vehicle he drove and what made him tick. If he drove the right kind of vehicle, Mr. Prayer Meeting might soon be standing in the need of prayer himself.

21

EINSTEIN'S NOSE

THE ADULT IN ME DECIDED it was time to tail my prime suspect; check for unusual activities or suspicious behavior. Hopefully, it would either clear Tim Dandurand completely or provide evidence I could present to the police. The kid in me just wanted to see Legoland. Lana's kid couldn't join me because her adult had four Tai Chi classes to teach.

Early Wednesday morning I sat in my car alone, a few doors down the street from the Dandurand's primly landscaped home in Vista. Vienna Supreme coffee steamed up from my open thermos. To hell with the cup-and-a-half limit today.

I glanced in the rear-view mirror and noticed my hair looked particularly shiny and my skin glowed. The vitality was due to more than quality nutritional supplements. I now live each day with the possibility of a cancer recurrence. Life vibrates to a different frequency: more urgent, more passionate, more finite. Brushing Death's cheek, I feel the life force in every cell; attend the *"tick, tick, tick"* in every moment.

I pulled back from the mirror and checked the car clock.

Any moment now Tim Dandurand would leave this French blue ranch house for the drive to Lego Land. I remembered to notice: yes, there were roses in his garden. Good-sized Mr. Lincolns grew on either side of the front bay window.

The automatic garage door crawled open revealing a tan Ford Expedition with its engine running. Plenty of cargo room for nefarious purposes. Tim pulled out of his driveway and turned down the street. I ducked so he wouldn't see me. When he was halfway down the block, I followed.

The drive from the inland North County community of Vista to the seaside town of Carlsbad involved seven treacherous miles on highway 78, a road I strive to avoid. It's boring, heavily trafficked, and has a high accident rate. This morning I had no choice, but I took the precaution of securing my thermos, unwilling to drive 78 one-handed.

I stayed two or three cars behind Tim as we exited 78 and merged onto I-5 south. We drove a few more miles, then took the Cannon Road exit marked with conspicuous Legoland signs.

When we got to Legoland he lost me. Employees accessed a special entrance and parking area, past the gatehouse. Without the proper ID, I couldn't get in. I know these complications never deter Elvis Cole or V.I. Warshawski but they certainly impose themselves on me.

I pulled into guest parking, locked my car, and walked to the entrance, only to be confronted by a row of massive concrete balls that looked like Stonehenge gonads. I wondered about them for a moment, then realized they served a practical purpose. Someone driving a large car could blast right through turnstiles, but not many vehicles could plow through concrete spheres. Maybe the Legoland entrance was designed the year some meth freak stole a tank from a National Guard unit and drove it through San Diego streets.

I entered the line to buy my admission ticket. Ahead of me two small Japanese boys restlessly tugged at their mother's blouse, trying to endure the long wait. The line moved so slowly that I wanted someone's blouse to play with, too.

Finally, ticket in hand, I passed through the turnstile and looked around. Within the park, everything shone red, blue, yellow, green, brown, black, gray, or white. Primary. Geometrical. Cutesy, but cutesy created by the same Viking descendants who brought you *I Am Curious Yellow*. Uff dah.

I knew Tim Dandurand worked here as a maintenance manager. I wasn't sure where to find him without alerting him to my presence, so I figured I'd just walk around until I spotted either him or located the maintenance department.

I bore left and was greeted by Lego-constructed elephants spouting water from a stream. The park flyer informed me I was in Safari Trek. Farther upstream zebra-striped Safari cars drove through islets of pampas grass where Lego ostriches and alligators marauded. I relaxed my guard a bit; this was going to be fun.

I drifted in that direction for about forty-five minutes, enjoying the rest of Safari Trek, Fairy Tale Brook, and a Lego train. The only real disappointment was that Driving School—a racetrack with electric Lego cars—would only accept drivers up to age thirteen. Ageism sucks; I'd really wanted to get my Lego license.

I was running out of amusements in this direction and hadn't seen a single maintenance person, so I backtracked toward the other side of the park. A Mindstorms sign up ahead piqued my curiosity.

Decorating the front of the Mindstorms building was a huge portrait of Albert Einstein composed entirely of putty gray Legos. It was a damned good likeness, too; amazing what you can do with those things.

I sat on a bench in front of Einstein to take it all in. That's when I noticed a flutter above his mustache. There, blending in against the plastic, perched a mourning dove. What would your politics, your religion, your stock market choices be if you looked at the world from the perspective of Einstein's nose?

When the dove flew away, I moved on past a smoking Lego dragon. From there I entered MiniLand where twenty million Lego pieces are assembled into detailed replicas of the Big Apple, Washington, D.C., San Francisco, and other landmarks.

I finally sighted someone who looked like she might know about park maintenance. She was trimming and weeding what I supposed were bonsai bushes in the San Francisco exhibit. "Excuse me—could you tell me where to find Tim Dandurand? He's a maintenance manager," I inquired of a slender woman in her late 50's who ignored my question and continued to tend the bonsai as though her life depended on it.

I repeated my request at a higher volume, just in case the kids screaming on rides had impaired her hearing. She looked up from under the brim of her sun hat. "I'm with Landscape. Maintenance is over there." With a small trowel, she gestured vaguely in the direction of a roller coaster.

After ascertaining that you could, indeed, build a miniature Chinatown with Legos, I headed for the roller coaster. I wandered in the vicinity for almost an hour and took two rides, but I never did find the maintenance department.

I polished off a late lunch of burger and fries at the Technic Test Track Diner, glad to get off my feet for a while. By midafternoon I'd been entertained, but was no closer to finding Tim Dandurand than when I entered. I asked a young man emptying trashcans what time the maintenance shift ended. Four o'clock.

By 3:45 p.m. I was parked along the road that leads out of Legoland, watching for Tim's vehicle. I don't know in what peculiar internal chambers (no doubt composed entirely of Legos) he'd spent his day, but at 4:17 p.m., he drove by.

Traffic was so congested that we averaged all of ten miles an hour on the freeway. Highway 78 was even slower. I was just about to resign myself to a reasonably amusing but unfruitful day when Tim took an exit, drove four blocks south, pulled in to a 7-Eleven parking lot, and entered the store.

I followed at a distance, parked on the street near the 7-Eleven and backtracked on foot. I hid behind various vehicles as they pulled in and out. Twelve minutes later my target had still not emerged. The essence of 7-Eleven's being "fast," I decided to investigate. Inside the store soft drinks, pretzels, chips, candy bars, laundry detergent, magazines, and lottery tickets were present. Tim Dandurand was not.

22

REMEMBER
THE PRETENDERS

I WALKED UP EVERY AISLE of the store, twice. I scanned the parking lot. The Expedition was present and accounted for, unlike its driver. I took the opportunity to see if the vehicle had gold carpeting. The windows were tinted and it was hard to be certain, but the interior carpeting looked beige. I returned to the store and approached the charitable looking Bombay native at the cash register. "Where are your restrooms?"

He handed twenty lottery tickets to a skinny girl on roller blades and spoke to me softly, "Our restrooms are not for the public. One block north, a public library."

I nodded and left. So much for Tim hiding in the john. I checked a nearby phone booth and circumscribed the building. No Tim.

7-Eleven's, to the best of my knowledge, did not feature trap doors leading to subterranean bomb shelters. Nor did I think they served as CIA safe houses, although Roark could find out easily enough. How the heck could a man enter a store in broad daylight and simply disappear? For lack of a better plan, I pulled my car into the 7-Eleven lot, turned on the sound system, and waited.

My favorite FM station was mainlining on commercials, so I popped in a Gabrielle Leatheross CD. Halfway through the first song—the one about thunderstorms Gabrielle had sung at the concert—urgent signals again tried to reach my conscious mind from some vigilant substratum. I could hear an inner message but I couldn't decipher it. I felt like Jodie Foster in the first hour of *Contact*.

By the time I'd moved on to k.d. lang, Tim had reappeared. He wasn't alone.

Following him through the 7-Eleven door into the parking lot was a beautiful young woman. She looked old enough to vote for president but too young to remember the Pretenders.

When they reached Tim's SUV, he turned to her and took her hands. They faced each other; I had them in profile. She gazed steadfastly into his eyes. I had no doubt that, given the chance, she'd wipe the hairs from the sink after he shaved and save them as love tokens. He gave her a quick good-bye hug, climbed into his Expedition, and started his engine.

I wondered if Tim had modified Exodus 20:14 to read, "Thou shalt not *admit* adultery." Maybe Cody had discovered the affair and threatened to tell Marilyn. If Cody was into near-jail bait, maybe they were both after the same girl. Romance can move in incestuous circles; ask any lesbian.

I followed the girl back into the 7-Eleven. She stood for a moment gazing out the window as Tim pulled away, then she kissed the cheek of the man at the register, and passed through an Employees door.

My face must have looked pretty baffled as I approached Mr. Bombay. "Excuse me, but who's the young woman that just went back there?" I asked, indicating the Employees door.

Pride and pain mixed in his smile. "She's my daughter."

"How does she know that man? The one with the thick blond hair."

He handed Lucky Strikes to a pot-bellied fellow in a sweat suit who really *needed* those cigarettes, and turned back to me. "Why do you ask these questions?"

"I'm a Community Liaison with the San Diego Police Department. Mr. Dandurand is involved in one of our investigations," I lied through my pearly whites.

"Ah, yes, I have heard about this. His wife's ex-husband was murdered, true?"

"Exactly. Now, what was he doing here?"

He rang an unseen buzzer. His daughter, head low, reappeared. "Take the register for me for few minutes, please, Kamla?"

Kamla quietly took over and her father led me into the back office.

"Mr. Dandurand comes to pray with my daughter several times a week."

I waited for more.

He offered it. "She fell while using the parallel bars in gym class her freshman year at college; the head injury caused lesions in her right frontal lobe. The same kind of brain damage Mr. Dandurand has from his construction accident. They met in a patient support group at the hospital."

"Dandurand has brain damage?"

"Surely you've noticed. His voice is very flat—that's called aprosody. His face shows no emotion; that's athymia. Kamla has many of the same symptoms."

I hadn't really gotten a good look at her face but I believed the tears in his eyes. "So?"

"He knows what she's going through. He's been courageous dealing with his own injuries. He is a good man, full of faith. They pray together, for their own healing and on behalf of others."

"You don't mind that he's alone with her?"

He smiled with eyes that seemed very wise for a 7-Eleven merchant. "I'm grateful he comes; it helps Kamla. And besides," he gestured toward the main store, "when they are together, I'm only a few yards away." He put his hand on the door. "Please excuse me; it's a busy time for the store."

"Certainly. Thank you for your cooperation."

He took over the register and Kamla, whose beautiful but vapid face was now more evident, disappeared into the back once more.

I revved up the Silver Bullet and shortly thereafter, pulled back onto I-5 for the drive home. My best suspect was rapidly turning into a saint rather than a sadist. And my only other viable suspect had skipped town. I hate it when that happens.

23

QUESTION QUARTET

"I HAD A LONG TIME TO THINK about it on the drive home—forty miles worth—and I've come up with four." I removed the hard-boiled eggs from the stove, ran cold water over them, and continued my conversation. "Questions, that is. You see, Raj, I don't think I can make any real progress until I have the answers."

Certain conversations are considered privileged—penitent to priest; client to therapist; anyone on Lana's massage table to Lana. My talks with Raj approach this sanctity for me. You can tell a pet your most asinine drunken stunt, your eighth grade shoplifting experience, and any one night stands you cleverly omit from your repertoire, and your pet will still love you, will still lick your face with the same mouth used to explore a decayed lizard carcass (or worse). No wonder we love them.

I sliced the eggs into a spinach salad, added croutons and dressing, and popped open a ginger ale. "What are these questions, you ask? Well, first I'm wondering if Tim's brain damage could lead him to violent or split-personality behavior?"

Raj finished the last vestiges of Science Diet in his bowl, and turned to consider my conversational points.

"Next, Kari says a doctor confirmed Ned Sowkopf's disability, but what kind of confirmation did they get, eh, boy? Did they get confirmation from the doctor in person, or did they just get a call?" I had Raj's full attention now, especially since he smelled the eggs in my salad.

I continued after swallowing a big mouthful of spinach. "Another thing why does Real Bob need money? Maybe if we knew that, we could find him. And last but not least . . ." I rubbed Raj behind his ear. "What if Cody never told Marilyn he had a child by another woman? If she found out, would she . . .?"

Raj gave a little bark; this latter line of questioning obviously disturbed him. "Why do I want to know that? Because I'm trying to look at all possibilities."

Raj looked skeptical but offered no immediate insights.

Hard-boiled eggs and Popeye fodder behind me, I looked to the future, "What's for dessert?"

I'm sure my yearning for sugar and carbs is a genuine biochemical addiction. One of these days I'll check myself into a retreat for carb addict rehab. Why not? Immaturity, prejudice, and stupidity seem curable by rehab. Surely it can do something for folks like me who find daily life more of a kick when it includes bear claws, ravioli, and Rocky Road. I searched the kitchen.

My brain chemistry led me to a pint of Jamocha Chip. Sitting at the computer with a bowl carefully balanced between my lap and the keyboard, I checked my e-mail for updates from Roark.

He had sent transcripts of the Somerville, MA, police department's interview with Berkeley Havrel. The young man claimed he had only seen his father twice in his life and that he was an architecture major at Tufts University. Beyond that, Berkeley refused to cooperate and threatened to lawyer up if detained. The lead detective noted that the boy seemed to have no knowledge of his father's bequest.

I was pondering the implications of this when the phone rang, startling me and nearly sending Jamocha Chip all over the floor.

"This is Tess."

"Baby Girl! What're you doin' home on a Wednesday evening? Isn't it 70's Night at The Flicker?"

"Roark-meister!"

"You need to get your bootie out there, woman! You're sittin' around playin' detective instead of spreadin' sunshine on the sheets of some sweet young thing," he chastised.

"'Sweet young thing?' Hah! If I want a soul mate, I'd best date women who have a personal acquaintance with perimenopause! What've you got for me, Boy Wonder?"

"It's taken a while, but we finally located something on Real Bob's lawsuit."

I sidestepped Pookie. "Spill it, big guy."

"Real Bob consulted an attorney by the name of . . . ." I heard Roark shuffling papers, then he came back on the line, "Uh, William Bearheart on March 2, regarding five songs for which he apparently feels entitled to royalties. The songs are all currently copyrighted by Cody Crowne."

"I don't get it, Roark. IPoGS can tell me whether or not

the president of Bulgaria used deodorant this morning. Why was this info so hard to find?"

"Real Bob never instructed Bearheart to file the claim; he merely consulted him about it. So there was no court record to find. And Bearheart isn't Real Bob's regular attorney. Even IPoGS takes a while to infiltrate the offices of all the lawyers in Los Angeles . . . ."

"Don't tell me any more; sorry I even questioned it." I trembled to think of how many attorneys' suites and intranets IPoGS had transgressed getting me this information.

"I gotta go; got an Antonio Banderas look-alike waiting for me. Later, wifey."

When I hung up the house phone receiver, I remembered I'd recharged my cell phone and decided to check my voice mail. Soon I heard: "I do not like green eggs and ham, I do not like them, Sam I am, but I kinda like you. I'll be in San Diego this weekend; call me if you'd like to get together. You've got the number."

I played back the message three times. Each time I heard Nova's voice, the breadth of my smile increased. I found her phone number and called immediately. I reached her voice mail and left a "you're it" phone tag message.

I returned to perusing my notes on Cody's murder and recorded my four questions. The one about Tim's head injury should be easy to answer. I Googled a search and scanned the abstracts of medical journals and case studies that appeared. Twenty minutes later I knew Tim's injury would not provoke crucifixion impulses.

I had just decided to tackle the next question when I heard them enter.

24

DUMPSTER DALLIANCE

IN THE DOORWAY, LANA AND GABLE were so immersed in mouth music that it took them a moment to notice they weren't alone.

It may take a worried man to sing a worried song, but it takes a lesbian to see men as they really are. I'm unimpressed by spicy aftershaves, rich tenors, hairy chests, or the willingness to change flat tires—things that can charm my straight female friends.

I don't hate men; I'd miss them badly if they weren't around. I just don't happen to find them as intriguing in the realm of long-term romance as women. I don't paint my toe-nails, I'm pushing fifty, and I haven't worn a bikini in years for damned good reasons, so chances are most men wouldn't find me all that intriguing either.

All of which leads to my assessment of Gable. I was in the man's presence for two minutes and I knew he was exception-al. Bright, fit, and at ease with himself, he made fabulous eye contact, and had an equally fabulous smile. I could see why Lana was attracted. Damn it.

The housemate part of me envisioned Lana married and moving out, leaving me with the entire mortgage to pay on my own. The ex-lover part of me imagined Lana exchanging unlimited bodily fluids with Gable, curdling me with an unidentifiable emotion. The friend part of me felt guilty for how the housemate and ex responded.

Threatened, curdled, and guilty, I endured a brief bout of small talk, then secluded myself in the kitchen with Tanqueray on the rocks until he left twenty minutes later. Like a child showing off her new Christmas toy, Lana bounded in as soon as he left and asked, "So what do you think?"

I struggled to think of a compliment I could offer that wouldn't drip hypocrisy all over the kitchen floor. "Uh, his Mars in Scorpio is quite evident and um, he seems smart and has a great smile."

Unfortunately Lana is highly attuned to what's not being said. "You didn't like him?" she thrust.

"What's not to like?" I parried.

"Tess, this is me you're talking to. What did he say or do that put you off?" She made herself a cup of tea. When I didn't answer, she sat down at the dining room table next to me, looked me right in the eyes, and waited.

I sighed, "OK; he's remarkable; the guy's a keeper. If you wind up marrying him, that'll mean some big changes in our relationship."

She rinsed her cup and said, "That works both ways, you know. You could be the first to find someone."

Being a spiritual tenth-grader, I'd never thought of it that way.

As she walked by me to go to her room, she tousled my hair and said, "I love you, kiddo."

The next morning, Lana and I arrived in the kitchen at the same time. A scarcity of breakfast options greeted us as we stared inside the fridge. No milk, no bagels, no cottage cheese, no fresh fruit. Two stale slices of whole wheat bread. I spotted a covered dish and handed it to Lana.

"Maybe we could have these. Lily made them for you."

She peeked under the foil and saw the lumpia. With a catch in her voice, she said, "I'll warm them up."

It was the first time we said grace over a meal in years.

After breakfast we headed to the local Wild Oats, a natural food grocery store. Forty-five minutes later as we walked to our car laden with bags of organic produce, whole grains, soymilk, teas, hormone-free meats, and other goodies, Lana suddenly stopped us in our tracks.

"Look!" She pointed to the Dumpster near the rear of the building.

"You want me to look at a trash bin?"

"Next to it, on the right." she whispered.

Near the Dumpster, a handsome okapi nosed through discarded onions. Although it kept a wary eye out, it seemed content, like a child staying at Grandma's for the summer who knows things are not quite like home, but who likes Grandma's cooking.

Slowly we approached the young animal, admiring its dark chest and striped haunches. We were mesmerized.

"What should we do?" I asked quietly.

"Nothing. It seems to be doing fine without our interference." She started back toward the car and continued, "I think the okapi's a good omen, Tess."

I fired up the car and we waved good-bye to the critter as we headed out of the parking lot. On our way home we sang along to an oldies station. We were mumbling the words to "Every Breath You Take" when Lana exclaimed, "Oh my God!"

"What's wrong?" I asked, thinking she'd decided we had to rescue the okapi after all.

"I'm not sure, Tess, but . . . do you remember when that song came out?"

"'Every Breath You Take'? Around '83 or '84, I think. Why?" I inquired as I scooted through a yellow light.

"Cody had a song out at the same time. I remember because I wondered why people made such a fuss about Sting and the Police when Cody had a better voice."

Although I disagreed with her assessment, I decided not to dispute Cody's vocal skills. Instead I parked in front of the house and popped open the FX's hatch. We grabbed our groceries and carried them in. Plopping them on the kitchen counter, I turned and asked, "OK. Cody had a song out around the same time The Police released 'Every Breath You Take.' And so? Fill me in; I don't get it."

"Tess, it's the lyrics. I'm not sure, but as soon as we put these away, I need to check something. "

"I'll put the groceries away; you go do what you have to do."

She went to the living room stereo and rummaged through her music collection. I was just finishing up when I heard her say, "Damn!"

I poked my head into the living room. Lana sat surrounded by dozens of CDs, scattered chaotically all over the floor. "What's wrong?"

"I can't find the lyrics insert for this CD." She held one in her hand. She began humming and murmuring a song to herself. The tune sounded familiar. At last she asked, "When you found Cody's body, was he facing a canyon wall or looking out toward the ocean?"

"Toward the ocean; why?"

"Then it must tie in somehow. But I need those lyrics!"

"Um, if it'll help, Roark sent me a discography list for Cody. It probably has all his song lyrics on it."

"Let me look at it." She seemed very animated and I sensed her urgency.

I found the discography file and handed it to her. She flipped through it and found the lyrics to Cody's song, "C & S," copyrighted in 1983. She handed me the CD. "Play track four, 'C & S.'"

We listened as Cody sang: *"I'm missing my tips; I'm longing for sips / But bear the cross I must / I gaze out to sea / Weigh the penalty / For it's C & S or bust."*

Lana continued, "He wrote it about a bartender friend of his who realized he was an alcoholic and was trying to get clean and sober. Remember? He sang it at the concert."

Of course. Maybe that's why those subliminal alarm bells had rung when I listened to the song on Gabrielle's CD that she had sung at the concert. "This is too much for coincidence; this is plain creepy," I remarked, going over the lyrics in my mind. "The 'bear the cross' reference is obvious, and tips must mean his fingertips," I thought aloud.

"And remember what the dentist told me—I can only *sip* for several hours after my next appointment? Without teeth, or with smashed teeth, you have to sip!" Lana exclaimed.

I was too full of adrenaline to sit so I stood up and paced. "What do you know about the bartender this song is written about?"

"Nothing really. I just remember Cody explained the song's background once in an album note or maybe in a TV interview or something."

"We've got to find out everything we can about this. If only we could get in touch with Real Bob." Then it struck me: was this song cited by Real Bob in his lawsuit?

I skimmed through Roark's files. The attorney had only noted song titles, not lyrics, but sure enough, "C & S" was one of the songs Real Bob claimed to have written.

It looked to me like Real Bob was in real deep shit.

25

PARSLEY, SAGE, CHIPOTLE, AND DILL

THE NEXT DAY FELT LIKE it'd been thrown into a blender on the Chop setting and seasoned with chipotle.

That morning a new SDPD report from Roark informed me, "On Weds., an Infiniti FX registered to Tessa Lynn Camillo tailed prime suspect T. Dandurand, purpose unknown. Same woman reported discovery of C. Crowne's body at Torrey Pines Reserve. Also note cross-ref on Camillo address; same as woman questioned in murder of L. Cabigoa. Connection? Involvement?"

This Camillo woman sure sounded suspicious.

The report, signed by Detective Bernais, made me wonder for the first time if there could be a real link between the two murders. I e-mailed Roark for police reports on Lily Cabigao. When they arrived an hour later, I learned something new. The "religious material" found next to the body was an open King James Bible with one verse highlighted: II Timothy 2:23, "But foolish and unlearned questions avoid, knowing that they do gender strifes." Kick-starting synapses formed in Bible College, I tried to recall if the verse had any particular significance, but drew a naught.

Lana had awakened with a fever and chills. She'd cancelled two massages, and was intermittently watching TV, sipping hibiscus juice, and sleeping. Every hour or so, I asked if she needed anything but otherwise I gave her a wide berth. Nancy Nurse I'm not.

When I checked on her during one waking spell, she asked me for a favor. Now, favors are a lot like treatment recommendations from your physician. You should listen respectfully, weigh the risks and rewards, and only agree to those that, in some knowing part of you, feel right.

Lana had promised to deliver Cody Crowne fan club memorabilia to a DJ for a tribute radio show, and she wanted me to make the delivery to the station for her. I listened respectfully and weighed the risks and rewards.

"Do you have it in digital format?" I asked. "Maybe we could just e-mail it to them."

She rubbed her aching throat. "These letters and things are from the mid-80's. I don't have them in 'digital format.'"

Her irked facial expression told me the rewards of doing the favor had just outweighed the risks, since the knowing part of me didn't want to live with a ticked off housemate. "OK, OK; I'll go." So the Silver Bullet and I zipped out into the drizzle of the day.

The barometric pressure was sponsoring a spitball contest. Just enough moisture hung in the air to make our oil-slicked freeways dangerous, but like everybody else, I cruised at 75 mph. That's what all-weather tires are for.

Situated near Aero Road and I-15, the Clear Channel Communications media complex housed nearly a dozen radio stations—everything from pop rock and hip hop to morning shows that featured conservative commentators like Rush Limbaugh and San Diego's own Wilbur Wedgelock. A sign near the main building read, "Finest City Broadcasting." The building featured unusual architecture with Coke-bottle green reflective glass walls, surrounded by pleasant landscaping. Although the complex held so many radio stations, I didn't see any radio towers, only microwave dishes. I guess broadcast towers are passé now that everything's done with satellites. Still, a radio station without a tower felt like an Italian bakery without cannoli.

To my left was an empty "Reserved for the Finest City's Finest" parking space. I decided I qualified as well as the next person and parked the Silver Bullet. I had my hand on the car door handle and was about to emerge, when I heard voices approaching. Guilty about taking the reserved parking spot, I slid down in my seat so I wouldn't be seen. The voices drew near, headed for the vehicle next to me. With my window cracked a few inches, I could hardly help overhearing bits of conversation now, could I?

A man's voice, rumbling in tone, urged, ". . . rapidly rebuilding my power base, Wilbur. But I need exposure."

A nasal male voice replied, "Next week we'll do the Soledad cross controversy. You heard about that rock star who got crucified? That's got people thinking about crucifixion and crosses again. Perfect time to review that whole Soledad mess. It'll be good exposure, Luke; lots of listeners."

I heard their vehicle's security system unlock. "Your stance is in keeping with my strict constitutional and states' rights views, so it'll be my pleasure. But after that, I want a forum on illegal immigration. That's my true . . ." The car door shut, ending my eavesdropping.

Realizing the men were oblivious about who was in the Finest City's Finest parking spot, I sat up and checked them out. Just as I'd suspected. As the black Buick Lucerne pulled out, I saw Lucas Zealeaux in the front passenger seat and Wilbur Wedgelock driving. Interesting. Sounded like Zealeaux wasn't going to let a little thing like a felony conviction impede his political career.

I dutifully delivered the packet of Cody memorabilia to the radio station. As I cruised back to my Mission Hills neighborhood, I wondered if I'd given enough consideration to the Soledad Mountain cross controversy. It was one of those issues that seemed to get everyone's bile a-broiling. I recalled that Sergeant Gonzalez had even mentioned it at the crime scene.

A 13-foot cross had been situated on Soledad Mountain in San Diego County since the '50's when the Mount Soledad Memorial Association erected it in memory of service members lost in Korea. (Jewish veterans be damned, as my mother would say.) Unfortunately, the cross sat on city property, which is what put people at, shall we say, cross purposes? As times grew more politically correct, lawsuits followed. The city attempted to have the property declared federal land, an effort George Bush supported. When controversy continued, the city sold the cross and the surrounding land to the Memorial Association. Nevertheless, the "Save Our Cross" campaign still titillates archrivals and triggers antipathy. I flirted with the possibility that Cody's murder might reflect a warped attempt to stir the controversy once more. And if so, how did that tie in with the song lyrics?

I'd been home only about forty-five minutes, tossing ideas around and tossing laundry into the washer, when a mental Eureka! came crashing to the fore. I reread the police report on Lily Cabigao, memorized her address, and headed back out to my car for the second time today, urgency nipping at my Nikes.

I sped up 805, turned west at the Balboa Avenue exit, north on Charger Boulevard, then made a quick right on Berwick Drive. Berwick looped through a well-cared for middle-class neighborhood, eventually running parallel to the freeway. A privacy wall stood between the freeway and Berwick, but it didn't provide much protection from the noise or car exhaust.

The sun was now breaking through, creating tiny rainbows in unexpected places. I got out of the car and walked around. Painted pale green with forest green trim, Lily's home was nicely landscaped with blossoming oleander and agapanthus. Yellow tulips grew near the porch, their optimism mocking the yellow crime scene tape that still blocked the front door. I thought of the little lumpia lady with her throat slashed and got a tight spot in my chest.

I paced two or three houses to the right of Lily's, then backtracked the same distance in the opposite direction. Most of the homes were thirty to forty years old and had been renovated. Lily had added what looked like a second-story master bedroom suite. Her neighbors had chosen to branch out, not up. On their properties I could see L-shaped additions with new stucco slathered on the outside of rec rooms and expanded garages. The neighbor on the right had even built a backyard gazebo.

I continued to walk the area. An old cat with a face like Yoda examined me from underneath a nearby Accord.

My suspicions were taking shape. Satisfied, I slid back into the Silver Bullet and returned home. I now knew who murdered our lumpia lady and our Holy Fool, but I didn't know why or how to prove it.

I wanted to share my new insights with Lana but found her dozing again. Back in my bedroom on the computer, I spent half an hour on Google trying to learn more about the bartender in Cody's song, to see if his identity fit my new theory. Focusing on music prompted me to put some oldies on the stereo. As I melted to Van Morrison, remembering bell-bottoms, incense, and the damaged countenance of boys just home from 'Nam, I felt twenty again. I felt young.

I also felt that the process of elimination is good for more than just the descending colon. To eliminate a nagging question, I asked one of Kari's underlings to check something for me. Ned Sowkopf's physician had indeed appeared at the station in person to give his statement and had provided copies of Sowkopf's medical chart.

All of this choppy, diverse information explains the Chop setting of my blender gestalt; Nova provided the chipotle.

I was folding laundry, listening to Simon and Garfunkle sing about culinary herbs, and refining my murder theory when my phone rang. "Hey, good to hear from you!" I exclaimed after recognizing Nova's voice. "How'd you like to help me solve a murder when we get together this weekend?"

"I usually don't *play dick* on a first date . . . . but tempt me."

I disentangled a lacy bra from a Velcro pocket tab on a pair of Dockers. "Woman, I'd love to tempt you—every way I know how. But I'm serious about the spadework. I need everything you can find on a song Cody Crowne wrote back in '83 called 'C & S.' I'm certain it ties in to his murder."

"Dill keeps musical archives. Don't get your hopes up, but whatever I find, I'll bring with me to San Diego. I'm at a producers conference all afternoon; can we do dinner?"

As I smoothed wrinkles from my clean laundry, we made plans to connect Saturday evening at Julio's Hacienda, a restaurant where the food's decent and the tequila anejo inspires indecency. My kind of place.

Hours later I handed Lana a fresh glass of juice and two Tylenol and left her watching a rerun of *Crocodile Dundee* while I walked the critters. Pookie sniffed every weed along the way and Raj stopped at a few dog taverns and tossed back a brew with his buddies. At least I think that's what he was doing.

I knew what I was doing; I was looking for the moon. I wanted her cool grace in my vision. I couldn't find her.

My mind wandered not to Cody's murder but to one of my personal mysteries—the mystery of how to handle my first sexual encounter since the mastectomy. I'd always been confident sexually but now things were different. In darker moments I realized this mystery had no solution that could be reckoned beforehand.

I eyed the night sky. Must be a new moon. Suddenly I knew that to seduce Nova properly, I needed a *Farmer's Almanac*.

26

LOST LANGUAGE

SATURDAY AFTERNOON I spent hours cleaning the house. Lana, still recovering from the bug she had, watched with curiosity and disdain.

"I didn't mop the kitchen floor before Gable came over," she snipped.

"I want everything just right."

"Whatever," she shrugged and left to practice Qi Gong on the patio.

I continued to futz. In my bedroom, I set matchbooks near candles and put clean sheets on the bed. I aired out the room. I placed all sexual toys and accoutrements in nightstand drawers within easy reach. Nothing more frustrating than not being able to locate lubricant or ben wa balls the moment you need them.

I went to Wild Oats for a bottle of champagne and a small crate of strawberries. In danger of becoming a *Penthouse* Forum stereotype, I showered, shampooed, and began the agonizing ritual of choosing the right clothes.

While I can relate to and enjoy the full spectrum of my sexuality including the most masculine and most feminine parts of myself, I'm usually more inclined toward my yang side and knew that was what Nova appreciated. Nix any lace or crinoline tonight. I finally settled on a pair of sage green carpenter jeans and a long-sleeve white cotton shirt with silver buttons.

I checked the *Farmer's Almanac* once more, happy with what it confirmed.

Lana looked forlorn when I said good-bye, so I gave her a hug, hoping I had immunity to any residual germs.

The restaurant was in Old Town, a historical preserve in the center of town that resembles a Zorro set. By 7:15, my Silver Bullet had ensconced itself in the Old Town public parking lot. I walked in right on time.

As my eyes adjusted to the cool darkness of Julio's Hacienda foyer, I saw Nova sitting on a bench. The feather eyelashes were gone and so were the slinky garments. In their place were black leggings and a luxuriant peach top with a shawl collar. The only visual reminders of our first encounter were the violet eyes and the white streak in her hair. We accepted a table out on the patio by the chimineria.

Half a margarita and some small talk later I exclaimed, "You're Jewish!"

She smiled. "When most people hear 'Zhenkarov,' they assume I'm a Russian Commie atheist."

"I knew I felt a certain, um, familiarity with you."

She licked salt from the rim of her gold margarita. "But— 'Camillo?' You're not Jewish, right?"

"I'm a demi-goy. Not to be confused with a demi-god, mind you," I teased. "My father's Italian. I get my passion from him."

"My mother's Venezuelan. We're not exactly frigid."

We exchanged a look; I lit the candle on our table.

"How did your Russian father find a Jew in Venezuela?" I wondered.

"He didn't. My mother was shopping in the L.A. garment district where he worked." The waiter brought our entrées. Nova looked up from the spicy food and said, "Renee—that's my ex—was a systems analyst. Do you like working with computers?"

"I see them as useful tools," I answered. You never knew when a woman might turn out to be a technophobe. Best to tread carefully.

"Was that your major in college? Computers?"

"My degree's in mathematics. Programming advanced algorithms was one way to turn my math degree into a paycheck." I crunched the last greens of my salad.

"Why math?"

Should I share with this violet-eyed music producer that algebra, calculus, and geometry inspire me with their beauty? That I hold a personal little ritual on Pi Day? Mention math at most female social gatherings and you're a pariah. Ask me how I know.

The tequila must have loosened my tongue; I took the risk. "I love math because it's a graceful, articulate language. Angles, spheres, relationships, sequences, probabilities—to me, they're downright elegant. I got hooked in high school my sophomore year when I learned how integral math is to nature. Fibonacci numbers in the spiral of a conch shell. The golden mean hidden deep in the flow rate of tree sap . . ." I realized I was rambling and stopped abruptly. I took another sip of my drink. "Teaching didn't pay much and accounting bored me; programming seemed a viable choice."

Nova tangled with a string of melted enchilada cheese, then leaned toward me and said, "Music and math have much in common."

"Patterns?"

"Patterns, complementary components, harmonies. Mozart loved math puzzles. He jotted equations in the margins of his compositions."

"Never knew I had anything in common with Mozart." Our toes started playing with each other under the table. Just a little rubbing and sliding and nuzzling.

I noticed she had a small birthmark on the right side of her nose. "Are you more interested in the production side or the music side of Dill's business?"

"I've loved music as far back as I can remember. I would have tried performing, but I've no tolerance for mediocrity, least of all in myself. For better or worse, I seem to have more talent for the business end of things." She looked off into the distance for a moment.

"How long have you worked for Dill?"

"Eight and a half years. He's the best in the industry."

Thinking of Dill, I suddenly remembered his archives and our mystery-solving mission. "Did you find anything on Cody's song?"

She seemed discomfited at the change of subject, but dug in her bag, found a sheet of paper, and handed it to me.

I read aloud, "The bartender was Kenny Albright; tended bar in San Francisco for five of the eight years Cody lived there. Nice guy but couldn't stay sober. Cody got him into a program. Dried out, went back to school; been working at Levi Strauss since '89." I looked up from the paperwork. "Guess Neil Diamond would say he's forever in blue jeans."

She cringed at the joke and gave me a little kick under the table. "How does this tie into Cody's murder?"

I explained the correlation between the song lyrics and Cody's death and disfigurement. She looked doubtful. "Maybe it's just a coincidence," she ventured.

"No, it's tied to Cody's death—I can feel it—but damned if I see how. I have some good police sources; I'll have them check this Kenny Albright; see if he's somehow related to the person I suspect. Maybe he didn't appreciate having his personal problems on the airwaves."

"You didn't know Cody, did you?"

I pushed my plate aside; there's only so much tostada you can eat and still be ready to rumble. "No, why?"

"Cody had integrity. He would never, *never* have written and released a song about someone's battle with alcohol unless he had their full approval."

"Didn't Cody have flaws? Everyone who knew him makes him sound like such a saint." I was genuinely curious.

She smiled sardonically. "He had a mediocre voice."

I slipped the papers into my pocket and raised my glass. Nova matched my gesture. "To Cody," I toasted. "May he now sing with the angels."

We finished our margaritas and paid the check. Out in the parking lot, I leaned over and kissed her lips. I was treading on romantic quicksand. I'd been there before; I recognized the squish between my toes.

She suggested we go dancing. She followed in her Audi TT convertible as I led us down Washington Avenue through Mission Hills and Hillcrest to The Flicker. They were hosting a Madonna event. The first song Nova and I danced to together was "Like A Virgin." Sometimes fate spreads the irony thicker than peanut butter on a Gracelandwich. We swayed and swerved and seduced one another to the accompaniment of margaritas and the Material Girl.

I wiped sweat from my face; it was a mistake to wear long sleeves dancing in San Diego, but they would come in handy soon. I checked my watch, then took Nova's hand. "Let's go."

She complied but when we were outside the bar she asked, "Why the sudden departure?"

"The grunions are running!" I answered as if that explained everything.

"Is that some sort of charity marathon?" she asked.

"Grunions are a kind of small whitefish like mullets, only they're silver. At certain times of the year and at certain tides, they come up to the high water mark to mate. Tonight's the day after the new moon—primo grunion-run time. There'll be zillions of grunions; you'll see."

"Zillions—now there's a precise mathematical term!"

We kissed again, and again I led the way, this time to La Jolla Shores. I could never hope to impress this woman who traveled in Hollywood circles with my material wealth, my career accomplishments, or with my familiar stocky looks. The only way I could impress Nova was to be myself—my earthy, non-Hollywood self. Grunion runs in no way resemble Grammy rites.

We parked and headed toward the beach. I held her hand as we climbed over sand dunes, down to where iridescent foam lapped the shore. I heard her catch her breath: mermaids had sprinkled the tidewaters with tinsel.

I'd seen the grunions run before but never so many. The wet sand shimmered like living mercury. Thousands of flip-flopping males offered their milt; thousands more females drilled their tails into the mud to burrow eggs. A piscine honeymoon was frantically taking place before our eyes.

I breathed deeply. The ocean smelled powerfully female. Nova spotted a fish stranded too high on the beach. She picked it up and ran it back to the water, squealing at the slippery sensation of fish in hand. As she rinsed her hand in the sea, her expression was like a four-year-old who had just gotten her first kite to fly.

After a while, the grunions returned to the Pacific and we returned to our cars. I leaned her up against my car and kissed her hard. She tasted salty, whether from margarita salt or sea air, I wasn't sure. "Come home with me tonight."

She whispered, "I no longer make love at every opportunity. Sometimes I like to let desire brew."

"You want to brew?" I put the warmth of my mouth over her left nipple through her top and sent a very personal steam around the areola. I kissed her throat. She began whispering lovely, naughty things to me that had nothing to do with green eggs and ham.

She pulled away and said, "Dill's company has a house on Sunset Cliffs; that's where I'm staying. Follow me there."

I didn't have to be asked twice. "I'm right behind you."

"Good, I like that position."

The old and nouveau hippie community of Ocean Beach adjoins the old money sector of Point Loma. Where they meet, a short span of sandstone cliffs directly overlooks the Pacific. These are the Sunset Cliffs. You can't live much closer to the ocean unless you're in a houseboat.

On the drive over, I phoned Lana and told her I probably wouldn't be home tonight.

When Nova pulled up, I recognized the house because I'd met Dill there once to do some business. A colossal Spanish mansion with a priceless view, it featured turrets, stained glass windows, a marble staircase, and a generous balcony.

The drive had cooled us down a bit. Nova led us up the staircase to a study and fixed us potent margaritas from Dill's private bar. The room was dominated by a white piano like the one Dill had in his Burbank home. She walked around, like she was trying to decide something. I studied Dill's eclectic decorating touch—jars of brightly colored jelly beans, framed handwritten sheet music for a piece by George Harrison, Danish sculpture, Maori masks. I thought back on the evening's conversation.

"You mentioned an ex—Renee. How long has it been since you broke up?"

I wanted to know if I was dealing with fresh wounds, although Nova didn't give that impression.

She turned toward me. "We didn't break up. She died in a fire four years ago." She spoke rapidly, trying to get it all out before I could ask. "Her condo building. They found out it was arson."

"I'm sorry." What else can you say?

Nova asked, "How about you? Has there been anyone in your life lately?"

"Not since last year's breast cancer. And mastectomy."

Nova leveled those violet eyes at me in quiet comprehension. After a few moments, she sat down at the piano and began playing a plaintive song of high complexity. When she'd finished the piece, she sat quietly on the piano bench. I walked up behind her and touched her hair.

"Should I recognize that? It sounded like Sarah McLaughlan or maybe Enya."

"I wrote it."

I leaned down and kissed the back of her neck. I began to wish we were back at my place. There was no comfort of the familiar to ease our first-time tentativeness. I'd done all that cleaning and fussing for nothing. I'd have to toss out my well-laid plans and concentrate on making Nova a well-laid woman.

Moments later she led me to the guestroom she was using, pulled back the covers, and started shedding clothes. I followed her lead as far as I could, but stopped short of removing my undershirt.

I pulled her to me. We lay there a while, holding one another and kissing. She felt almost as delightful as she smelled. Nova slipped from the bed, went over to a dresser, and returned wearing her feather eyelashes. Slinking down over me, she pushed my shirt up a bit and tantalized me with those feathers, brushing butterfly kisses all over my belly. In areas where my abdominal nerves had been bisected, I had no sensation, but where I could feel, it was lusciously ticklish.

Soon bed linens—300-count white cotton with tiny rosebuds—intertwined with shoulders, knees, breasts, and lips. Eventually I entered her from behind and took her deeply for a long time.

When we changed positions, her softest inner layers became the rink in an Olympic competition; my tongue, the skates. I played with figure eight's, smooth glides, and occasional double Axels. Encouraged by her moans, I won the Gold with a triple loop.

Afterwards we wrapped a sheet around us and sat out on

the balcony holding each other, listening to the ocean's rhythm. She murmured dreamily, "Maybe math is the lost language of Atlantis."

"Or maybe music is."

The last image I recalled was a bedside alarm clock. I spooned her close and hoped she hadn't set it.

27

RISKY BUSINESS

I AWOKE TO RINGING IN MY EARS. I slapped the alarm clock a few times. The ringing persisted. I sat up and saw that Nova was no longer in bed. My head felt like a blowfish. Tequila makes you want to dance on tables the night before and feel like an autopsy table the morning after.

Nova walked in carrying a breakfast tray. She put it down on the nightstand next to me, and handed me my ringing cell phone, retrieved from a pile of clothes on the floor. I saw aspirin on the breakfast tray and nodded thanks.

"This better mean I won the lottery," I rasped into the phone.

"Real Bob just called me; he wants to talk to me before he turns himself in." Like a wisp of smoke, Lana's voice curled through my ear. Somehow hearing it softened the throbbing in my head. How does she *do* that?

I tried my best to lasso some coherent thoughts. "Uh, why did he call *you*?"

"I gave him my card when we met up at Dill's. Says he

wants to talk to someone he trusts before he gives himself up. Apparently, I qualify. Would you like to go along?"

Although she didn't say it, I could hear the subtext in her voice: she wasn't comfortable meeting him alone. I chased the aspirin down with coffee. "When?" For the first time since I awoke, my brain actually registered the numbers on the clock face. It was 9:46.

"We're meeting at the Balboa Park carousel at eleven. Can you make it or should I handle this alone?"

"I can do it. Thanks for letting me know." I hung up and inhaled more coffee.

Nova emitted subtle distancing cues. No good-morning kisses; no lounging around in bed; just coffee, English muffins, aspirin, and a gentle smile from halfway across the room. Uh oh.

"Sorry, that was Lana with some news about Real Bob," I told her.

"Have the cops found him?"

"Not exactly. He wants to talk to Lana before he turns himself in."

"And you're going with her?" she asked.

I nodded.

"You and your housemate are going—alone and unarmed —to meet with a man who's wanted by the police in a murder investigation?"

"Well, it's not as bad as it sounds. We're meeting at a public place. And he already told Lana that he trusts her. Besides, it's not the first time I've dealt with a murderer." I trailed off when she sat down on the bed in front of me and looked at me with eyes that could've come from a Cat Stevens song.

"You're making what I have to say so much easier," she began.

A different kind of alarm thumped in my chest.

She continued, "I'm old enough to know what I want and I'm willing to take certain risks to get it. But some risks, I won't take. I'm more fragile than I used to be." Her hands picked at the rosebuds on the sheets.

"Well, I'm old enough to know how and too old to know better. Why does this feel like good-bye when I haven't even kissed you good morning yet?" I asked, hoping against hope.

She stood and paced. I drank more coffee and nibbled the English muffin. Sunlight the color of margarine poured in. My head pain had subsided a bit, but my heart pain was just beginning to rev. I'm usually awake for hours before my day is this screwed up.

"Last night meant a lot to me, Tess. That's a problem. I can't fall for someone like you just a little. If I let myself fall, I'll fall hard. You're the real McCoy."

"I thought Real Bob was the real McCoy."

She refused the distraction. "You're too high of a risk, sweetie. You've had breast cancer; there could be a recurrence. I could deal with that if you didn't compound it by chasing criminals around like it's a hobby. If I let myself fall for you then lost you, I couldn't stand . . ." Her voice broke.

I took a couple deep breaths and thought about what she said. I was high risk; how could I deny it? If the shoe were on the other foot, would I go step on a nail?

"So, last night . . . that's it?"

She stopped pacing and came near enough for me to catch her scent. "Not necessarily. As long as I don't see you too often or let myself get serious."

I pulled her to me and baby-kissed the birthmark near her

nose. "Why don't you have a hangover? You had at least as much tequila as I did last night."

She laughed. "I've been up since dawn. I've had three aspirin and two Bloody Mary's."

Then she leaned close and kissed me—slowly, luxuriously—the kind of kiss that's meant to cover many months and many miles.

28

RIDING FROGBACK

FACING BREAK-UPS AND sleuthing murderers are relatively facile endeavors compared to finding a parking space in Balboa Park on a beautiful Sunday in spring. Southern Californians just don't get the concepts of carpooling, mass transit, or hoofing it. Our cars are extensions of ourselves (myself guiltily included) and too many egos were extending where I wanted to park. The drive from Ocean Beach had taken thirteen minutes; finding a parking space took another twelve.

On my way to the carousel, I spotted Real Bob's tan Dodge Ram pickup in the next row of vehicles and walked over to check something. Peering through its windows, I could see that the interior carpet was gold, just like the carpet fibers found at the crime scene.

The carousel was housed in a structure of the same architectural flavor as those sketches of the original Globe Theatre you've seen in books about Shakespeare. Painted an unappealing combination of yellow with brown, cream, and beige trim, the result is Tudor meets gruel.

Lana sat on a park bench near the ticket kiosk. "Where's Real Bob?" I asked.

"Not here yet."

"His truck's here," I asserted.

"Well, I'm sure he'll see us. Meanwhile, let's take a ride!" she suggested.

Sounded good to me; I could use a little pick-me-up. We bought our tickets and waited for the carousel to stop. As it unloaded, we checked the passengers. No Real Bob.

On the carousel, horses, giraffes, lions, tigers, frogs, spotted pigs, striped zebras, orange ostriches, and at least one green dragon pranced with pride. Most were originals, hand-carved by craftsmen. Many of the horses sported genuine horsehair tails.

In the center, brightly colored murals in the style of Gay 90's cigar boxes decorated the upper walls. Below the paintings, the center walls enclosing the carousel's movement mechanism were encrusted with beveled glass jewels and mirrors.

I wanted the green dragon, but some kid beat me to it. Lana straddled a zebra; I found a giraffe. Soon a bell clanged, signaling the start of our ride. Breezy classical music played. Some animals moved up and down but the zebra and giraffe had no inclination to pump two forty-something women into the air.

The music grew upbeat and powerful, as did the G-force pushing us toward the outside of the carousel. Each time I passed the carousel manufacturer's placard, I tried to read it. After four rotations, I finally knew it was made in 1910 by Herschell-Spillman of North Tonawanda, NY. All of this information made me a richer person, but I was still poverty stricken when it came to Real Bob's whereabouts.

When our ride ended, Lana insisted on treating us to another one. While she bought tickets, I walked around the carousel enclosure looking for Real Bob. Meeting Real Bob seemed as tricky as meeting Godot.

This time Lana and I selected two green frogs with bright saffron seats situated next to each other and behind a four-seat sleigh. Lana's shoulder bag slipped off just as the starting bell rang. She dismounted her frog and tried to retrieve it but the carousel began moving. She landed on her derriere.

A young female ticket taker watched Lana scrambling on the floorboards, chewed her gum, and calmly asked for my ticket. I handed it to her and she smiled. "Here for the long haul, huh?" she asked knowingly. I wasn't sure what she was talking about, but I returned the smile. Lana finally pulled herself up, saw me smiling, and elbowed me. Hey, a frog rider's gotta do what a frog rider's gotta do.

When the ride ended, I dismounted but Lana stayed on her frog. "I bought us Super tickets—we get to stay for another ride!"

Spinning carousels don't combine well with barely mitigated hangovers. I was deciding if my stomach could take another round of spinning when a bushy head of orange hair popped up from behind the back of the sleigh in front of us. Real Bob was wearing a gold T-shirt, blue jeans, moccasins, and dark glasses. He'd shaved his beard yet still managed to look unkempt. Part of his charm, I suppose. Like a flame-haired Bozo, he fit right into the menagerie around us.

"Sorry for the runaround, but I wanted to be sure no cops were lyin' in wait." Real Bob looked at me. "Do I know you?" he asked.

Before I could respond, Lana told Real Bob I was a friend helping her clear her energy concerning Cody's murder.

"Sit with me," Real Bob invited, patting the sleigh bench. "There's room. Otherwise we'll have to scream." We obliged.

He began by directing a comment to me: "I better be able to trust you." Then he looked at Lana. "You're the only one who asked me how I felt about Cody's death, and seemed to care. You didn't treat me like a suspect; you treated me like a human being." He looked down, making it difficult to catch his words as we twirled around. "I didn't kill Cody. I want ya to know that. I owe the wrong people a lot of money; it's made me do some dumb ass things. But I didn't kill Cody." He was now speaking directly to Lana, ignoring me.

Lana used New Age-speak to assure him that we were all going to work together for the best possible "karmic outcome." I kept my mouth shut and listened.

"I have this gamblin' problem," he began. He went to stroke his beard, realized it wasn't there, and found his chin instead. "It started years ago; I'd go to Vegas, Reno. Back then, Cody and me were haulin' in some hefty diñero. I could afford to indulge. I won plenty at first but, I don't know, after a while our concerts weren't drawin' as many people; albums weren't sellin' as good. But I couldn't stop bettin'; in fact, I gambled more. By the time we were an opening act, I was borrowin' off Cody. When he realized I was just gonna blow it all on blackjack or craps, he stopped loanin'."

A small but imperious girl on a white horse in front of us spanked its haunches in an effort to speed things up. My stomach wanted to slow things down. Lana asked, "Where've you been hiding?"

"I got in some trouble in Vegas, so for the last few years I been hangin' at the reservation casinos here in East County—

Sycuan, Barona, and Viejas. When I needed to disappear, members of one tribe—rather not say which one—let me stay with them, livin' beneath the white man's radar. But the other day they found out I owe money to some of their tribal council; I've worn out my welcome."

"But if you didn't kill Cody, why hide from the police in the first place?" Lana asked. The merry-go-round stopped; people dismounted.

The three of us finally left the ride. I was glad to get my feet on something that only moved around the sun once a year. Just beyond the carousel at one end of the parking lot, a landscape designer with little respect for parking space utilization had created a large circle of grass. In the middle grew a coral tree, fiery blossoms weighing down its branches. Lana and I sat under it on the shaded grass; Real Bob paced nearby.

"The cops found out I was threatenin' Cody with a lawsuit," he said. "They also know I stayed in my Del Mar condo the night he was murdered. As far as they're concerned, that's motive and opportunity."

"And you don't have the money to hire a lawyer?" I prompted.

This time he looked at me when he spoke. "I barely have the jing for an oil change, let alone a lawyer." Suddenly his tone changed. "Hey, I remember you—you were at Dill's party, askin' me questions."

Lana touched his arm solicitously. "She's OK. Like I told you, she's a friend."

Real Bob shook his head as if it were against his better judgment to trust me.

There was something I had to know. Observing him closely I began, "You lie. You evade. You hide. You act guilty. I think you really feel guilty. Why? You think you could've prevented Cody's death somehow?"

He looked at Lana. She nodded, "Your heart chakra will stay blocked until you choose to clear it."

Eyes to the ground, he answered, "I tried to cheat Cody; that's why I felt—feel—guilty. One of the tribal elders knew this attorney who, well, let's just say ethics aren't his strong suit. They knew I needed money; this shyster convinced me we could shake Cody down for some sizable bucks—enough to pay off all my gamblin' debts—with a copyright lawsuit. He was willin' to work on contingency, so it wouldn't cost nothin'."

"Did you actually co-write those songs with Cody?"

"Nah, I gave 'im ideas how to pump up the rhythm and lay out the percussion, but Cody wrote the songs. The casinos were pressurin' for their money and I was still convincin' myself to go through with it when Cody was murdered."

And Cody left his only Grammy to this guy. Criminitlies!

Staring at the carousel, I watched a mother secure her toddler to the back of a tiger. I remembered the same kind of leather straps securing my waist on a boardwalk carousel in Atlantic City when I was young.

We were making progress with Real Bob, but it was time to dig deeper. "One of the songs in your lawsuit was "C & S." Why that song?"

"That was the lawyer—William Bearheart's—idea. Bearheart said it'd be too obvious if my lawsuit only cited songs that made big bucks. He told me to include one or two that didn't do all that well. 'C & S' and 'Raleigh's Cape' were supposed to throw off anyone who thought I was suing just for the money."

In its own greed-inspired way, the explanation made sense. "OK. What else can you tell us about the song? We know it was written about Kenny Albright. Was Albright ever hostile to Cody because of that song?"

Real Bob looked at me like I was the original one-eyed, one-horned, flyin' purple people eater. "Hell, no! Albright loved Cody. Cody helped him get his life straightened out. Albright made Cody godfather to his kids."

I kicked at the grass. I was missing something, some piece that would link the song with the person I thought was the murderer.

Real Bob leaned down and whispered, "There's this guy who keeps looking over here. I think he's a cop. I gotta split."

Lana and I looked where he indicated toward the far end of the parking lot. Several families and couples were milling about, but I didn't see anyone who looked threatening.

"Where?" I asked.

"Over there, near the VW van. Guy's wearing a jacket. Why the hell would you wear a jacket on a warm day? He's hiding his gun."

I followed Real Bob's gaze. A black man was leaning over, examining something on a license plate. His back was toward me, so I saw more butt than face. It seemed like a non-threatening butt.

I didn't see anything to worry about so I continued, "Anything else about the 'C & S' song that was unique from the other songs you and Cody performed?" I asked.

"Lemme think." Real Bob was nervously ducking into the

tree's shadows, darting glances this way and that. He'd be perfect for the role of Paranoia in his school play. Finally he offered, "Only thing I can think of is it was the first song where the profits went to charity. See, Cody had recorded the *Bayberry* and *Random Winds* albums right before that, which sold really good; made a shitload of money. He decided anything over a certain amount was going to charity. "C & S" didn't bring in great bucks, but everything it did earn Cody donated to Project GoodFight."

Real Bob finally sat down next to Lana and turned to her. "I could really use one of those neck rubs of yours," he pleaded.

Lana kneeled behind him and began making mojo with her fingers. In her most persuasive voice she urged, "You said you were thinking seriously about turning yourself in. That would be the enlightened thing to do. You're stressed to the max. If you cooperate with the police, there'll be less negative energy all around. Just tell them you don't have the money for a lawyer and they'll get you one."

Real Bob seemed doubtful. "They'll gimme some dipshit right out of law school. I'll fry."

Suddenly Bernais and an underling appeared from the other side of the coral tree and began reading rights. "Robert Simpson McCoy, you're under arrest for the murder of Cody Crowne. You have the right to remain silent. Anything you say can and will be used against you . . . ."

Real Bob had been right about the man with the jacket. "How'd ya find me? Did these broads set me up?" he demanded.

Lana objected, "I would never do that!"

Bernais answered, "Actually, we've been following Ms.

Camillo. Wanted to see what she was up to. Finding you with her was a real break. On your feet, pal."

Real Bob covertly handed something to Lana and whispered in her ear. Then he stood up and offered his hands to Bernais for the cuffs.

Lana gave him a quick hug; Bernais gave him a shove toward a squad car.

As soon as the cops left, I asked excitedly, "What did he give you?"

"This." She held up a twenty-dollar bill. "He asked me to put it on a third round KO by the champ in next Saturday's welterweight match in Vegas."

29

JUNE CLEAVER'S KITCHEN

ALL THAT FRESH AIR at Balboa Park handed my appetite a megaphone. "Lunch at the Chicken Pot Pie Shop?"

Lana nodded. "Sounds good. I haven't been there in a while." She had biked to the park, so we chucked her bicycle in the hatchback of my Infiniti and rode together.

The Chicken Pot Pie Shop has been a fixture in San Diego since FDR lusted for Lucy Mercer. The food is deliciously old fashioned—creamy, comforting, and highly caloric. A five-minute drive got us there. As soon as we walked in, ceiling fans wafted aromas toward us that might have come from June Cleaver's kitchen on Ward's birthday.

The décor was *Green Acres* kitsch. We stood in the entranceway waiting to be seated. Nearby hung a white ceramic tile painted with a black cow and the admonishment, "Eat Chicken." A high shelf along the far wall held ceramic poultry of every sort. Rhode Island red knickknacks could be found behind the cash register; macaroni art of leghorns and bantams hung on the dining area walls. Not exactly Martha Stewart, but with food this good, who gives a cluck?

A hostess seated us in a small booth. Lana and I scarcely looked at the menu, opting immediately for the traditional pot pie, a garden salad, and iced tea. As soon as the waitress had taken our order, Lana observed, "You believed Real Bob when he said he didn't kill Cody?"

I nodded agreement. "And you?"

"Uh huh. I remember when I did the massage at Dill's, his body tension was high when he talked about needing money, but relaxed when he talked about Cody's murder. His story seems believable. But he was the only link with the 'C & S' song. Where does that leave us?"

We hadn't had a chance to catch up for several days. "Lana, I'm almost sure I know who murdered Cody; what I don't know is why or how I can prove it."

"Maybe I can help." She dripped ranch dressing on her salad.

"One of the first things Sergeant Gonzalez said at the crime scene was that it would take more than one person to pull off the crucifixion. Tim Dandurand could've done it with the help of the men from his prayer group, or with his wife, but I have no reason to think he's got any bad intentions. You yourself actually gave me the best clue." I savored the hot creamy innards of my pot pie, licking my fork.

"I did?"

"Yes. You told me to look for someone who was truly evil."

"So who did it already?" Lana asked, doing equal damage to her entrée.

I'd awakened to a hangover and romantic disappointment. I'd already spent a chunk of my day looking for parking and listening to Real Bob defend his behavior. When I got home, it was my turn to clean the dog poop out of the back yard. Gloating in my detective work was likely to be the high point of my day. I wanted a room full of suspects, à la Hercule Poirot, in which to make the guilty party squirm. I wanted a spotlight and solemn stillness. Instead, I got a room full of chicken gravy, waitresses, rattling plates, and rooster art. Must've been a real bad-ass in some past life to catch this kind of karma.

When Lana's fork had come in for a landing, I began. "Think about it. Once you eliminate Tim Dandurand, who else could have had help to commit the murder? And who has a really dark soul?"

"Well, this bartender guy, he might have been at the concert with a friend. And he could be very evil. We don't know anything about him," Lana suggested.

"Nova gave me some info Dill had about the bartender. It jives with what Real Bob told us. From what I can put together, the bartender's not our guy."

"Well, then, who?"

I took a long sip of my ice tea, spat out a lemon seed that had slipped its way up my straw, and declared, "Lucas Zealeaux."

"Lucas Zealeaux? But the Highway Patrol officer vouched for his alibi. I don't see . . ."

"They're in it together, Lana. I still don't know why, but it fits. Zealeaux is capable of cold-blooded murder—he fried a whole van full of people just because they were from south of the border; never showed the least bit of remorse. What clinched it for me was the murder of Lily Cabigao."

"That's tied in somehow?"

"If you drive by Lily's house, you'll see—it's the only home along that stretch of 805 that's a two-story. From the second floor she could see over the privacy wall that separates the homes in that neighborhood from the freeway. Lily—and only Lily—could have had a clear view of whatever transpired between the Highway Patrol officer and Lucas Zealeaux. Why else would someone like Lily be murdered? The Bible verse left near her body—it was about asking questions. Zealeaux was afraid the police would ask Lily questions about what she saw that night."

"Good God," Lana muttered. I could visualize her playing mental chess with various suspects, motives, and possibilities. "Did you check on his vehicle?"

"Yup. The DMV database shows tags issued in his name for a white Ford Econoline van. Plenty of room in the back," I answered.

Lana shook her head stubbornly. "That 'C & S' song's not just coincidence. Every ounce of my intuition tells me it ties in somehow. Could the bartender be related to Zealeaux or the Highway Patrolman?"

I finished my iced tea and flipped over the check. We owed less than we would have paid for two McMeals. Long live the Chicken Pot Pie Shop! I turned back to Lana. "I don't honestly know how the song fits in, but I'm going to find out."

She looked wary. "You're going to the police with this, right?"

"Not yet; not without evidence. To accuse a respected CHP officer of involvement in a murder, I need hard physical evidence if I want to be taken seriously. Otherwise, all I'll do is tip off the murderers."

"What're you going to do?"

"I'm going to pay Mr. Zealeaux a little visit. But first, I'm going to go home, talk things over with Raj, and see what he thinks."

30

SWEET POTATOES

LOUISE LIFTED HER HUSBAND'S *tan uniform shirt from the laundry basket and examined the perspiration stains. She sprayed the underarms with stain remover. From the utility room, she called to him, "John?"*

He walked in from the den, holding today's newspaper in his hands. He'd been reading the paper every day from front to back, something he'd never done before. "What is it?" he said with deer-in-the-headlight alarm.

"Darling, look at these stains. You never sweat like this before in spring. You're nervous about something. You're up half the night. I don't know if you're getting any sleep. What's going on? I'm your wife; you can tell me. Are you in some kind of trouble?"

John felt a bountiful tenderness toward Louise rise in his chest, only to be countered by self-disgust. He looked at her warm autumn eyes, classical cheekbones, the trim curves of her body, and he wanted to vomit. She was a good woman, and he had brought a heinous hellhound into their lives. Louise could never begin to understand. Zealeaux had damned well better keep his word. He wanted nothing more to do with that son-of-a-bitch.

"I'm just distracted," he told his wife. "I know they're evaluating me for the job in North Carolina. It would be a promotion; a much better environment for the kids. Plus, I take the lieutenant exam next month; I've been staying up late studying."

She gave him a look. "You're full of crap, John Bartholomew Barkovic, but I love you. When you're ready to talk, I'm here." She tossed the shirt into the washing machine. "Ham and sweet potatoes for dinner tonight. Your favorite."

He hugged her and went looking for his anti-anxiety pills.

31

BREAKFAST
OF CHAMPIONS

MONDAY MORNING I WAS in the shorts and tee shirt I had slept in, eating kashi cereal with strawberries, drinking Kona Gold coffee, and reading the *San Diego Union* headline: "Fellow Musician Arrested in Cody Crowne Murder."

The phone rang and I picked up only to hear the familiar voice of my boss, Walker. "Are you building an ark?" he teased. "If you're going to be gone another week, you need to come in and fill out a leave of absence extension form or HR will have my butt." The tone of his voice turned ten degrees toward whiny. "We need you back soon. How much longer do you want off?"

"Another day or two. I've almost got everything worked out," I said.

"OK, don't forget to come in and sign the extension form. Take care, Tess."

Even over the phone connection I could sense he wasn't

thrilled with my absence, and was even less pleased with my secrecy. I had to be careful. I'd missed a fair amount of work last year when I had my cancer surgery and was probably on the short list for layoffs. I thanked Walker for his understanding, hung up, and concentrated on breakfast. After a while, the rasp of Raj's tongue tickled my bare leg. I reached down and did a little homo sapien-canine bonding.

When Lana eventually dragged herself out of bed, I was playing with Raj on the living room floor, sharing with him secrets about my night with Nova. Lana gave a surprised cough and crossed into the kitchen.

I returned to the breakfast nook, lifted my coffee cup toward her in greeting, and said, "Another day, another dollar."

She reached for an herbal tea bag. "I wonder, does 'another day, another drachma' have the same feel to it? Or 'another day, another yen'?"

"You really don't need caffeine to jump-start your freight train, do you?"

She looked at me quizzically, victim of our humor dichotomy.

"You have time to help me with something today?" I asked.

She glanced at her calendar on the side of the refrigerator. "Let's see, today's Monday . . . um, I teach Tai Chi from eleven to one." She spread marmalade on a whole wheat muffin. "Gable and I are meeting for dinner. I've got the afternoon free. Why?" She looked at me, then answered her own question. "You're not serious about going out to Lucas Zealeaux's, are you?"

"Serious as the Diet of Worms."

She made a weird sound. "A diet of what?"

I realized my reference to Martin Luther's reformation trial was a bit obscure. "Sorry, I had a Bible school moment. But yes, I am serious. I just need to nose around a bit. If Zealeaux murdered Cody, I'll find *something*—maybe the remainder of the rope he used—I don't know; something." I waited till Lana swallowed before finishing. "I need you to come with me."

She didn't choke. Instead she got up, walked across the kitchen, and poured Pookie and Raj their Science Diet. She hadn't said a word.

I poured fresh water in their bowls, set them on the floor, and turned to her. "We'll be careful, I promise. You're going to be my lookout; you'll have the cell phone. Just call the cops if anything happens." I was using my most convincing eyes; I wondered if she remembered some of the things they convinced her to try eighty-twelve years ago. I poured my extra half cup of coffee and awaited her usual litany of questions which would force me to see the foolishness of my ways.

The questions never came. "You got involved in this because of my fondness for Cody, so I'll do it. On one condition. I want to tell Gable what we're doing just in case anything . . . happens . . . and I'm late for dinner tonight."

"Great! Thanks, I really appreciate it." I cleaned up my breakfast dishes. "I gotta get dressed and head out. I have to stop by Imitech and sign some HR paperwork. Then I'm going to Project GoodFight. Real Bob mentioned that 'C & S' was the first song where the profits went to them. Might be something to it; worth checking. I'll be back to pick you up this afternoon."

An hour and ten minutes later I was propelling the Silver

Bullet east on Friars Road past a kudzu vine of condos, the IKEA-Lowe's-Costco complex, and Qualcomm Stadium. I continued past an under-construction culvert. The air smelled clean and the sky was a billboard for cumulonimbus vanilla sundaes.

The southern California regional office of Project Good-Fight occupied a second floor suite in one of those buildings that resembles the offspring of a warehouse and a Motel 6. At least there was plenty of parking. When I walked in, a young woman with magenta hair and severe dental problems smiled at me. "Hi, can I help you?"

"I hope so. If you keep records of your cases from the '80s, I'd like to take a look at them."

"Uh, let me check." She walked into the back of the office, tapped on a closed door, opened it, and went in.

In a few moments she returned, followed by a dark pleasant young man whose spiked black hair looked like he'd had a GoodFright. "I'm Mike Prabhakar—Regional Director of Project GoodFight. Our files here go back as far as 1982. What's your interest?"

"Tess Camillo; nice to meet you." I extended my hand and we shook. "I'm a programmer for Imitech Foundation." I handed him a business card. "We're creating a Web site for a historical society on significant legal battles in southern California. We can get most of what we need from public records. But we thought some of your files might add depth and color to the content." Lie only as much as you have to. After all, it works in politics.

Mike shrugged. "Look all you want, but nothing leaves the office." He motioned me over to a big metal file cabinet. "Our case files from '82 to '85 are in here. That ought to get you started. You can use this table if you want. Should you feel motivated to make a donation, we'd certainly appreciate that." He pushed an envelope into my hand.

I nodded thanks and began my search. A song copyrighted and released in 1983 would start making profits around 1984, I figured. Two paper cuts and seven manila folders later, I learned that the regional chapter of Project GoodFight had worked only two significant cases in '84. One had to do with alleged mistreatment of sea lions, who sun on the rocks in La Jolla Cove; the other provided help to the Assistant DA handling the Cougar Leap Canyon case. Bingo.

According to the files, the political mood of the time (rather like the current one) was not sympathetic to "illegal immigrants." Zealeaux had been a rising political star until his arrest; putting him in the limelight as a criminal would embarrass people in positions of power. So the Assistant DA decided to bury the case in a mound of paperwork, let the publicity die down, and when the time was right, plea bargain him to a slap on the wrist.

When Project GoodFight pressed him about it, he complained of insufficient investigator staff and a heavy caseload. I spent another thirty minutes reading every word of the file. Chills tingled. The money Cody donated directly provided the public scrutiny and legal muscle that put Zealeaux behind bars. "C & S" was responsible for ruining Zealeaux's life. At least I was pretty sure Zealeaux saw it that way.

I wrote Project GoodFight a check for $20.00, tucked it into the envelope, handed it to Purple Hair/Yellow Teeth, and headed home.

By the time I opened my front door, I had it all planned how two unarmed perimenopausal women would do what all the king's horses and all the king's men hadn't been able to. Then I fell over Pookie.

32

GRUESOME TWOSOME

"I'VE BEEN SCREWING AROUND with this case long enough. It's been over two weeks since I've played poker, gone to a movie, or read a good book. And believe it or not, I actually miss work," I rambled to Lana. "It's time to get down to business and nail this sick son-of-a-bitch."

"Do you have to use the word 'nail'?" she asked while I opened the sunroof.

"Nails would be too good for him. He should be dipped in a vat filled with sulfuric acid maybe," I mused.

"Tess, do you think maybe you've gotten a little obsessed with this?"

"Nothing wrong with obsession, as long as it's temporary. They call it 'focus.' Chronic obsession is what gets you into trouble."

Lana and I had departed about 2:15, after she'd called Gable and left him a message. If she didn't meet him for dinner at the City Deli at 7 o'clock, he was to call the police and inform them of our adventure.

Dust swirled in the bright afternoon sunlight along Buford Road in the suburb of Pesado where Zealeaux owned an isolated five-acre spread. The smells of black sage, coyote mint, and wild fennel punctuated the air. Live oak and alpine willow cast patches of shadow, and billows of mountain laurel graced my view as the Silver Bullet sped by.

Lana's truck would've blended into the community better than my Infiniti. Northeast of San Diego and southwest of the Laguna mountains, Pesado is Margaritaville's answer to Nashville. Pesado folk liked big trucks, rodeos, loud music, racetracks, old-time religion, and conservative politics. I didn't go there much.

About two-hundred feet from Zealeaux's, I pulled over and parked in the shade of an old sycamore. We got out and locked up. "Now remember," I told Lana, "if anything happens, if you even *suspect* something is wrong, call the police immediately. You've got Kari's number, right?"

"Right. Hey," she added, laughing nervously, "I'm 'Guarding Tess.'"

I chuckled. "It worked for Shirley MacLaine." Under my breath I added, "And you and she have a lot in common."

"OK," I continued. "I'll go see if the coast is clear. If it is, I'll snoop around the garage. If I can get into his van, I bet I find something worthwhile."

She looked at me full on and I'd never seen her look lovelier. True courage does that to a woman. I drew my breath in; made myself exhale to relax. I decided we'd better do this now before one or both of us came to our senses. I gave her a quick hug. Lana slunk behind a clump of broom bush growing where Zealeaux's driveway met the road. I crept toward the stucco ranch house.

The day seemed too beautiful for our actions. People don't risk their lives tracking murderers when the sun warms the body and the air soothes the lungs. They do it in alleys and bars and abandoned farmhouses in the rain in the dark when the sun has agoraphobia and the air smells like an ashtray.

No dogs barked; a lone horse whinnied far in the distance. I crouched behind an overgrown hibiscus and peered through an open living room window. Quality maple furniture. A blue braid rug. Gold-framed print of an American eagle over the fireplace. Zcalcaux was snoring in a plaid recliner. In front of him, ESPN broadcast a golf tournament. TV golf is better than Sominex. I decided it was safe to try the garage.

The two-car garage was detached and set back about ten yards from the house along the gravel driveway. I backed down the driveway, keeping my eyes on the house. No sign of movement.

I tried the garage side door and slipped inside. Good ole boys don't lock garages out here in good ole Pesado, I guess. A white Econoline van took up half the space. The sight of it evoked the same reaction in me that the taste of eggplant does: I gagged. This is where Cody had been tortured. I don't know how I knew, but I was certain. I tried its doors; the van was locked.

The garage was surprisingly clean and smelled faintly of Pine-Sol. A workbench and tool rack wrapped around most of the interior. To the far right stood a washer and dryer; next to them, a utility sink. Between the laundry area and the workbench sat a cabinet of plastic storage bins with sliding drawers. I checked them, hoping to find aluminum gutter spikes that forensics could match to those used in the murder. I found several kinds of nails as well as screws, drill bits, bolts, and washers, but no spikes. No yellow nylon rope either.

I reached inside my jeans pocket for one of the Baggies I'd brought with me. I'd once seen a murder solved by soil samples on a forensic science TV show. Maybe the soil at Torrey Pines Preserve was different from soil here in Pesado. I dropped to the floor, crawled under the van, ardently wishing I was a size 6 instead of a 16, and began scraping dirt samples from the undercarriage and bagging them.

That's when I heard the commotion.

I scooted from under the van and peeked out the garage door. A CHP car had pulled up out front. A tall dark-haired officer was berating Lana, pulling her by her elbow from behind the bush.

The ruckus awakened Zealeaux, who opened his front door and snarled, "What the hell's going on out here?" He looked down the driveway, saw the car, and began walking toward them. "Oh, it's you," he said to the CHiP. "And who do we have here?"

Officer John Barkovic explained, "I found her snooping around out front. Do you know her?" He jerked Lana by the arm again. The hard lump in my throat refused to move when I swallowed.

Zealeaux gave Lana a good long look. "I like the picture but don't recognize the canvas," he smirked. He turned toward Lana and said, "This is private property, Miss. What are you doing out here?"

Instead of answering, she reached for the cell phone. She'd managed to punch only one or two digits when Barkovic knocked it out of her hand. Shit.

"I don't like the looks of this, Luke. There's a Infiniti parked up the road; odds are, it's hers. I'll run the plates." He cuffed one of Lana's hands to his car, walked out to the road to read the plates, then recited a romeo, tango, zulu incantation into his radio. Moments later he received a static-laden response. He clipped the radio back on the dashboard and conferred with Zealeaux. "Car belongs to Tess Camillo. Recognize the name?"

Zealeaux's expression changed. "She found the body."

"Quite a coincidence," observed Barkovic.

Zealeaux turned toward Lana. "So you stubbed your toe on Cody Crowne, huh?"

Lana began singing very softly under her breath. Or maybe she was praying.

Zealeaux said, "Let's get her inside."

Barkovic uncuffed her from the car and together they walked her into the house, passing from my view. I bent down low and scurrried to the cell phone lying in the dirt. I pushed the On button. The phone was dead. I banged it a bit, in case it was related to those vending machines that revive when physically abused. The phone remained as unresponsive as a bureaucrat the day before retirement.

I could run back to my car, drive to the closest neighbors and use their phone to call the police. But what would I say? "Oh, Officer, come quick. We were trespassing and breaking and entering when a law enforcement officer detained us. Hurry!"

Even if I could convince the police of the danger in our situation, the nearest neighbor might not be home. If I had to go to several houses, it would be a while before help arrived. It was about three-thirty; most folks would be at work until after five. I was afraid to risk it. I crept back to my window post. The wind blew a branch into my hair, triggering an adrenaline-filled quiver. If this kept up, I'd have to change my underwear when I got home.

With handcuffs and rope, the two men had secured Lana to a dining room chair. They questioned her, but she continued to sing: "*You took me down to the wire / Fueled by my fire / Left me more alive and a-loved.*"

Her voice was a little louder now; I could hear her clearly.

"This man is an officer of the law. And he happens to be a friend of mine. You were trespassing on private property. You want him to arrest you? Take you to some filthy cell to be held overnight? Is that what you want? Answer me!" Zealeaux screamed at her.

"*Hard enough for winning; soft enough for losing / The pain is my companion / I've learned to like the choosing / Meet me at Bayberry and Fourth; Bayberry and Fourth / We'll hold each other against the rain on Bayberry and Fourth.*"

Lana's singing voice sounds different from her speaking voice, but both are richly melodious. Her lilting rendition of Cody's song served as a strangely positive counterpoint to Zealeaux's accusations.

Suddenly, Zealeaux had had enough. He backhanded her hard. She looked up at him, vulnerable as a babe at breast. Blood seeped from a split lip onto her yellow blouse. Trembling, she said, "I don't know what you want from me. I'm not who you think I am."

If she hadn't sat there singing Cody Crowne songs, they might have believed her. After all, she wasn't Tess Camillo; they could hook her up to a lie detector and she'd pass with flying colors. Too bad neither of us had invented a good cover story beforehand.

Barkovic shifted his weight. "Look, Luke, I came over here to tell you I've been accepted for a position in North Carolina right outside of Winston-Salem. The last thing I need is to stir up trouble right now. I just want to get away and forget. Look at her; she won't cause any more trouble. I'll escort her back and make sure she gets on the freeway." He moved toward Lana.

Zealeaux stepped between them. "We'll crucify her! I've still got some 2×4s and . . ."

Barkovic's head snapped toward Zealeaux. "Are you out of your mind? Watch what you say!"

Lucas's face now revealed his Lucifer. Eyes that had been so merry and blue in Kari's interrogation room and so ambitious at the radio station now brimmed with malevolence. "Think about it, John. They'll think 'serial killer'; there'll be less scrutiny of the Crowne case in and of itself."

Perspiration dotted Barkovic's forehead. "No! It's an overreaction. It's stupid. I . . . I . . ."

Zealeaux made himself comfortable in his recliner and smiled. He looked quite normal again, more jaded politician than Mephistopheles. He focused on Barkovic and spoke so softly that I had to lip read. "You think you can't do it. But you can. We understand each other, maybe too well, John. The same dragon breathes its fire in both our veins."

"Don't be so sure, Luke. I hated owing you, but I paid your asking price. I'm done with that." Barkovic's hand moved toward the shiny black holster at his hip.

Zealeaux pushed the footrest of his recliner down slowly, stood, and walked toward Lana. "Tennyson wrote, 'Man's word is God in man.' Our word is our honor; keeping our word gives us integrity, isn't that right, Ms. Camillo?"

Through her terror, Lana appeased him with a nod.

He continued, "This big brave officer of the law—he perjured himself. In sworn testimony." Zealeaux drew Lana's attention to the thick gold ring he wore. "Only graduates of Valorum Academy wear these." Zealeaux then pointed to Barkovic. "Look at his hand."

Barkovic made no attempt to cover the identical ring he wore.

Zealeaux continued, "I've never known anyone who loves his work more than John. He lives and breathes law enforcement." Zealeaux paused, scrutinizing the CHiP. "But when he was nineteen and we were roommates at Valorum, he got drunk after a midterm celebration and drove his Pontiac over a five-year-old girl." Zealeaux smiled at Barkovic and continued, "Big brave John hit and run. He came crying to me in the barracks. We sanitized his car and I alibied him." Zealeaux turned back to Lana. "He sold his honor to have an honorable career. Although the irony is delicious, Tennyson would have disapproved. Big John owes me."

"*Owed*. I *owed*. I've paid, remember? Cut the crap, Luke," Barkovic ordered. He was circling Zealeaux and Lana. The room seemed to shrink when exposed to his muscular pacing. I ducked each time he passed by the window.

Zealeaux looked at Barkovic as though he were a slow-witted child. "You paid, true, but I just raised my rates. Maybe I was an oil company in my last life." He laughed delightedly at his own joke and began untying Lana's ropes. "We'll take her out to the garage to do it. Less to clean up out there. Where shall we hang this one, I wonder? I saw a construction site near Grossmont Center the other day. Had a skyscraper crane. Maybe we could suspend it from that."

"It," not "her." Lana was already non-human to him. His demented ego depersonalized her the same way he had depersonalized nineteen "illegal aliens" dying in the desert heat.

I turned away from the window and was about to run for the car to get help when I heard it: A quick, shuddering explosion. Then, an unnatural quiet. I moved back to the window and looked in. Blood, bone, and something that looked like whale ambergris were spewed all over the braided rug. Barkovic's hand still held his gun, but as he lay dead on the floor, I didn't think he'd mind anymore if I borrowed it.

33

SANTA DEMENTIA

LIKE A SANTA WITHOUT A CHIMNEY, through the window I flew like a flash, ignoring the shutters and almost threw up (not the sash) when I landed face down on the soiled rug. Zealeaux would need a few seconds to adjust to his accomplice's suicide and that someone who looked nothing like Superman had just flown through his window.

I sprang up, grabbed the gun, and pointed it at Zealeaux. "This ought to be good for life in San Quentin." I learned to shoot when I was in the navy, and unlike my pacifist friends, have no qualms about using a gun when necessary. Brandishing the weapon like Bogart, I directed him back into a corner of the room. All I had to do was keep him at bay and call the cops. "Where's your phone?"

He walked over to an end table, picked up a phone hidden from my view by the angle, dropped it on the floor, and stomped on it. Those shards of plastic and wire would no longer let me or E.T. phone home. This guy was slimier than the reeds under a duck's butt. I should've shot him right then and there.

I moved next to Lana. "There must be another phone around somewhere in a house this size. I'll free you, then you find it and call the cops. I don't think it's a good idea for me to walk this guy all over the house looking for a phone. Loosen as much of the rope as you can; I'll find the handcuffs key."

I stepped close to Barkovic and patted his pockets. His body still emanated warmth and seemed at once horribly alive and very, very *gone*. A feral metallic scent permeated the air.

The key wasn't in Barkovic's pockets. His holster featured a handcuff pouch that might have a key holder. I took my eyes off Zealeaux for a second to unsnap the pouch.

What unsnapped instead was my head. White currents of pain took a NY taxi ride through my skull. I rolled over and saw Zealeaux standing over me with the gun. As Grandmother Camillo used to say, "Faccia brutto illumina di ege!" Roughly translated, and without the Abruzzi accent, it means, "What an ugly face in the light of something or other" or less literally, "Shit, it's you."

Zealeaux didn't seem thrilled with me either. He looked down at me and preached, "So stupid! So misguided! Don't you know that every time someone interferes with my mission, this country becomes less and less what our forefathers died for? If Project GoodFight hadn't gotten in the way, I would've returned to state politics and pushed my agenda through. The rest of the country would've followed California's lead. Thousands of lives would've been saved at the Twin Towers. Terrorists are all immigrants, after all. I'm the one man who can prevent this nation from being decimated by immigrant riff raff. Now you've interfered." He glanced toward Lana, then looked back down at me. "It'll be a bit more challenging, but I think we can still have a crucifixion—maybe two. Get up!"

I slipped my hand in my pocket, grabbed the Baggie of dirt, and flung it into Zealeaux's eyes. Forensic proof that he'd driven to Torrey Pines Preserve seemed the least of my worries. The gun went off a few inches above my head. Lana screamed. I dove for his feet and pulled hard, knocking him to the floor.

We wrestled, crashing lamps, and otherwise redecorating the room in a manner that would appall Christopher Lowell. I tried wrenching the gun from his hand. Unfortunately, a 6' man who'd been bulking up in prison was more than a match for my chunky 5'5" post-cancer surgery frame.

He managed to straddle me. I caught a glimpse of the gun as it blurred toward my head with force.

The next thing I remember was fighting waves of nausea from head pain as I came to on the garage floor. My arms were bound to a cross board; my feet tied together on a vertical board. My head was worse off than any of my limbs—so far.

I didn't like the situation one bit. If I screamed, he'd pistol-whip me again, and frankly, my skull had had enough. Besides, his nearest neighbor was a quarter-mile down the road. My only hope was that Lana might somehow loosen her ropes, find a phone, and call for help. I clung to that hope the way Christopher Reeve had clung to research on spinal cord regeneration. Then I remembered her hands were still handcuffed to the chair. No way she could untie those ropes.

For a man who had a dead cop's brains on his living room floor, and two women tied up on his premises, Lucas Zealeaux was a marvel of composure. He rummaged in his storage bins, taking his time, selecting nails. "Wish I'd kept a few of those gutter spikes," he muttered. "Don't think the nails I have here are big enough for the wrists. Have to use the palms."

Oh, God. I hadn't fully appreciated until this moment what a strange boon the blindfold had been to Cody. Knowing what this asshole was capable of made it even worse.

He crouched beside me, wincing slightly as his knees hit the concrete. He had the head of a large nail secured in his teeth. He removed the nail from his mouth, placed it in the middle of my left palm, and steadied it with his left hand.

I'd like to say I had the courage to rise above my own dilemma. I'd like to say I was heroic, but the truth is I would've done almost anything to avoid the pain I knew was coming. Fear blotted out the sound of birds chirping outside and the faint melody Lana was singing. Fear blotted out the smells of Pine-Sol, motor oil, and Zealeaux's aftershave. Fear blotted out everything but the pounding of my heart.

My tormenter looked me right in the eyes and down came the hammer!

Savage pain flooded me. Zealeaux seemed undeterred by my screams. "You're quite a chubbo. One won't hold your body weight," he scorned. "Better use three or four." He reached for another nail, positioned it, and raised the hammer again.

I first saw his chest implode, then I heard the bullet. Zealeaux slumped sideways to the floor. I heard Kari's voice yell "Call for paramedics!" and I passed out.

34

THREE TO ONE

AS PART OF MY BREAST reconstruction operation, surgeons had inserted five drain tubes in my body to prevent harmful accumulation of post-surgical bodily fluids. These tubes are Jackson Pratt, or JP, drains. These thin plastic tubes, some a foot long or more, come straight out of your flesh, like something in a Frankenstein movie. At the end of each drain is an oval-shaped squeeze bulb with a lift-off cap. Patients are supposed to empty the drains every few hours—see how much they're oozing and record it on a chart. I had tried to be a conscientious post-op patient, but the JPs drained me in more ways than one. They were, in fact, one of the biggest emotional drains of the entire ordeal.

My hand was now being held in a clamp, and a doctor was inserting a JP drain in the middle of my palm. I didn't want to go through this again. I would tell them "No, I refuse this treatment." I tried to pull myself up to protest. Movement dotted my forehead with perspiration and sent my motion sensors spinning. I lay back down.

That's when I awoke. It took me a few seconds to realize

that the JP in the palm had been a nightmare, but the medical environment was for real.

A young Middle Eastern man nearly sprinted in with a chart in his hand. "I'm Doctor Kasmirin; I've been treating your hand wound."

I tried to sit up. Felt sick. Lay back down. Dr. K had a nice smile. "Am I going to lose function of that hand?" I asked. First things first. But did I really want to know?

"You'll regain almost normal use of your left hand," he assured. "We lavaged the wound and repaired the tendons. There are no signs of infection. It'll take time, but usually a straightforward puncture wound like yours won't result in any significant loss of function. There's tendon, artery, and nerve damage but all of it will essentially heal."

Quite an optimist. I like that in a doctor. He looked down modestly. "Is there anything else you'd like to know, Ms. Camillo?"

"You single? I've got a niece who just turned eighteen."

He smiled and marked something on my chart. "You suffered a slight concussion, too. Try to get as much rest as you can," he encouraged and walked out into the hall.

As soon as the opportunity to have them answered was gone, the questions arrived. Which hospital was I in? Would I have to stay the night? Did my insurance cover it? How did Kari know to come to Zealeaux's?

I looked around the room, moving my head slowly. It looked like a pleasant private hospital room. Two flower arrangements lent cheer—one with bright mums and daisies; one austere and elegant in an Asian style. I found a TV remote, made sure the volume was set low, and clicked On.

A color TV on a retractable shelf brought the Channel 39 News to me. Something about the okapi being recaptured by the zoo. Oh, well. She would have adventures to tell her grandchildren about the exotic world outside the zoo—of inner city canyons, of Wild Oats Dumpsters, and of strange beasts called Chrysler and Toyota.

A few minutes later another news segment informed me that Real Bob McCoy had been released from police custody in light of new information about the Cody Crowne murder. Real Bob had crossed the border immediately thereafter. By now he was probably up to his overalls in Tequila Sunrises in the back room of a Tijuana gaming parlor.

My head was beginning to clear. It still hurt, but the nausea was subsiding. I heard the door open and in walked Kari.

"You sure are one sorry ass investigator," she began.

It was good to see her, but not quite as momentous as the last time. "Thanks for coming."

"Girl, you gonna have more visitors than you know what to do with."

"I didn't mean here. I mean, I appreciate this, but what I meant was, thanks for coming to the garage. How did you know what was going down?"

"Lana had set Gable's number to a speed dial, which she managed to punch before they knocked the phone away. Gable heard the call come through; he had caller ID, so he knew it was Lana. When the call was cut off abruptly, he decided something wasn't right and he gave me a call. Something you shoulda done, girl. You are *so* hard-headed."

"With both Zealeaux and Barkovic dead, I guess we'll never know exactly how they pulled it off."

"We've put some of it together," Kari remarked. "Zealeaux's alibi was bogus. He'd coerced one of his fanatical friends to lie for him. Zealeaux left his home, then probably drove north for a while on 805, and made a U-turn at one of the exits to head south again. That would make it look like he was driving home from Temecula. Exactly what Zealeaux and Barkovic did next, we can only guess. Forensics shows Cody was definitely crucified in the van. Barkovic probably hid his patrol car and rode in the van with Zealeaux, eventually helping him suspend the cross over the cliff. Then Zealeaux probably dropped him back off at his car and Barkovic resumed his patrol."

"There's something else I gotta ask, Kari." I was sitting up in bed now. I stretched so I could look all the way to the door. We were alone. "Did you warn Zealeaux before you shot?"

Kari took a piece of gum out of her pocket, unwrapped it, found the trash can, discarded the wrapper, popped the gum in her mouth, chewed a few times, and answered, "You know what we found on his property, Tess?"

I shook my head "No."

"Part of one of Cody's molars. In a vacuum cleaner bag. Got a preliminary DNA match. We also found clothes in his closet that match fibers from the Cabigao crime scene. I love legally obtained, incontrovertible physical evidence." She turned her back and walked away from me, toward the foot of the hospital bed. "You didn't hear me give him a warning?"

"Uh, frankly, no." My eyes still held the question; she saw that when she turned toward me again.

"If you're asking me for an official police statement, I most certainly did issue Mr. Zealeaux a loud verbal warning and he ignored it, leaving me no other recourse but to discharge my weapon at him. If you're asking me as a friend—Kari to Tess— maybe I decided to save the taxpayers some money."

She looked right at me with that last part and hugged me good-bye. "I'll be back with Sergeant Bernais a little later for a formal statement. Take care, Girl." I heard her words just before the click of the closing door.

I dozed off. I rested like I really needed it. I did. Once when I drifted awake, I wriggled the fingers of my left hand, and they worked. All except the ring finger, the one on which I hope someday to wear a commitment ring. The tendon between my hand and that finger seemed damaged, but it hurt less than I thought it would. Some sweet painkillers in my IV drip.

An LVN in an aqua top with Scripps Medical Center stitched across the pocket came in. She checked my IV, my pulse, and tidied the room. She didn't say much. I didn't feel real conversational myself.

I dozed again. When I awoke, I turned the TV back on. I was watching the umpteenth political debate of the season when Lana and Gable walked in. She had two neat little stitches on her upper lip. I teared up when I saw that. To stem the flood of emotion, I turned to Gable and said, "My hero!"

Lana gazed at him proudly. Gable grinned a grin that spoke of young girls, freshly mown hay, wagon rides, and full moons. How a metropolitan Feng Shui marketer manages to convey that charm, I don't know.

He didn't brag, so Lana did it for him. "You're lucky Gable was self-assured enough not to have to play cop himself. The fact that he called Kari probably saved your life."

"I know. I owe ya," I said as I shook his hand with my good one.

"And all of us owe the Fool in the Road," he replied.

A Zen aphorism, I guess.

He squeezed Lana's arm. "I'll track down the doctor and find out when Tess'll be discharged." Turning back to me, he assured, "Whenever that is, you've got a ride home."

Spoken like a man who understood hospital priorities. First: Make the pain go away. Second: When can I get out of here?

Lana took my hand. At exactly the same moment we asked each other, "So how are you doing with all this?"

I began, "Lana, I'm so sorry. About your lip. And all the emotional trauma; everything! You were right, it was stupid to . . ."

She cut me off. "Sshh. I'm OK; I'm OK." She smiled at me and I could see she really was OK. She continued, "Don't hold all this inside, Tess. I know usually you can handle life's ups and downs, but this is like the cancer. With some things it's just wiser to share the feelings." She let go of my hand and paced a few feet away.

"Speaking of sharing feelings . . . I've got some news. Gable's asked me to join him for a summer vacation on a farm-house in Provence!"

"Provence? As in France?"

Her smile grew like wild cucumber vines. "Yes. We'll be guests of some expatriate friends of his. They run a lavender farm." Her eyes brimmed with joy.

I caught myself feeling happy for her. Truly happy. The residual jealousy, which had been a pale stain on my heart, had finally been bleached clean by time. "Sounds fantastic! Do it!"

She knew I'd miss her. With her eyes, she thanked me for giving my blessing. "Lana, why did you sing Cody's songs to those assholes?"

"To keep them off-balance. I thought it might be just spooky enough to rattle them, but not threatening enough to make them hurt us," she explained. "I guess I was wrong."

"When you sang, it was like something of Cody was there. It was like having another ally against Zealeaux."

"That made it three to one—you, me, and Cody—against Zealeaux. No wonder we succeeded."

My math major mind turned to the notion of three. I hadn't had that "third wheel" feeling around Gable and Lana. An awareness, yes, but not the discomfort. Some hole in my heart had healed completely. Now I just had a hole in my hand.

In my Philosophy of Mathematics course—an elective I loved—I was made aware that we express the concept of "threeness" by writing a numeral that has a beginning, a middle, and an end.

At some point, every story has a happy ending. At some point in the journey, the guy (or girl) gets the girl and the girl still loves him (or her); the sun still shines; the flesh still heals; the heart still mends. Yes, every story has a happy ending, if you know precisely when to stop.

Tess Camillo returns in...

BLINDED BY THE LIGHT

Coming from Alyson Books Fall 2008
Turn the page for a sneak peek . . .

1

NO HAND BASKET
REQUIRED

BRISTLY BLACK LEGS of foot-long tarantulas crawling over your naked body. In a locked room. Forever. That was the personal vision of Hell of my best friend in high school. The unrelenting boredom of absolutely no sensory stimuli throughout eternity might be someone else's Hades. My own version of Hell would include Ron Jeremy, long hypodermic needles, and a looping soundtrack of the Oz munchkins. I'll spare you further details.

As I raised my living room blinds on this mid-June morning, I knew that, whatever Club Med of Misery lay beyond, it had a reservation with my name on it. What else could await someone who spent her morning nibbling apple butter on whole wheat, sipping Kona blend, and hoping for a murder?

Soft drizzle dappled the picture window. June is one of the few months when San Diego gets variation in weather, usually in the form of a heavy fog we call June gloom. This morning the weather was like an ADD woman at a shoe store. It tried on this; it tried on that; fog mists here; sunshine and sprinkles there. Nothing seemed to please for more than a moment. Suddenly, an angled shaft of sunlight lanced through the room.

Since my thoughts were already on Hell, I was reminded of Lucifer—the Morning Star, the Bearer of Light. I'd probably get to know him personally after wishing for murder. I didn't really want anyone specific to be killed, certainly not anyone I cared for. But in the real world, the Big Bad Wolf prowls. People do get murdered. And if it was going to happen anyway, I wanted to be tangential to the act, involved somehow in bringing to justice those who took human life. Synchronicity had enmeshed me in two murders already, and I was jonesing for the next adrenaline rush. My thrill thirst may have had something to do with the fact that my romantic and professional lives weren't exactly hot skittles at the moment.

As I stood there, a magnanimous rainbow shimmered across my living room floor, and danced along the Guatemalan rug. If a rainbow could dance, so could I! In fact, I could tango. I put the *Frida* soundtrack in the stereo and turned up the volume.

My housemate, Lana Maki, and I enjoy dancing together. Back before Jesus spoke to a president about the righteousness of invading sovereign nations, back when W 43 was just the coked-up scion of an ex-CIA Director, we'd danced a different dance together—the Great Dance that inspires all others. Lana was fey, Finnish, and feminine. And I fell. Hard. After dabbling in the lifestyle for a few years, Lana met a poet-boxer at her credit union one day, and soon made a withdrawal from my bed to his. Their relationship proved more haiku than epic, but it ended our affair. Since then we've lived together as housemates, moving through our lives with comfortable complementarity and a half-smile of things remembered.

The tango partner in my mind was Lana. The tango partner in my arms was an oversized bed pillow that never missed a beat. Step, glide, stomp! I snapped my head around to the beat. My pulse pranced and strutted along with the music—a *giro* here, a *barrida* there. All I needed was a rose between my teeth.

The rhythmic stomp of my feet was enough to dissuade my Welsh terrier, Raj, and Lana's intellectually undistinguished (that's the kindest way I can put it) dachshund, Pookie, from getting underfoot. Both dogs lurked in the kitchen, where they studied their food bowls as though the last few nibs of Science Diet were canine koans.

My fantasy dance was abridged by the ringing of the phone. When I noted the caller ID, I almost didn't pick up, but guilt poked me like one of Salma's high heels. My brother, Barry "the Baron" Camillo, was calling from NJ. The Baron had taken his family to Africa for a month; it would be rude not to welcome him home.

As I picked up the receiver, I groped the end table for pen and paper. The Baron has the habit of going into infinite detail on every little thing in his universe, and when your brain has turned to pudding from boredom, he'll shrewdly question you about what he just said. I'd learned to make notes.

"Oh, the smells! The rain—it's just so different, Tess. You *have* to go. You and, you know, one of those chicks you hang with—whichever one is the flavor of the month—*go*. Start with Tanzania like we did. On the first safari, we saw eight black rhinos—imagine! Eight! There're, like, maybe ten in the whole world. And . . ."

I sank into the creamy leather of my living room sofa. My "Uh huh" met his "and water buffalo—nasty suckers!" My "Wow" balanced his boast about how quickly he'd picked up pertinent Swahili phrases.

". . . and Brooke even got to fly one of those paraglider

things. We slipped one of the park rangers some American green, and next thing you know, there was my daughter—sailing over the African plains. 'Course, Bridget was so jealous she couldn't stand it, and turned into a total snot for the next three days."

As I stared at the living room fireplace, he came up for breath for a few seconds. I wondered if he'd asked me any-thing—anything—about my life. Ah, but there's a reason we nicknamed him the Baron.

He continued with fervor, "In Nairobi, we stayed in the Giraffe Manor. You actually feed giraffes from your hotel win-dow! They stick their heads right in! I swear, Sis, this trip was . . . well, you're just going to have to see for yourself."

I jotted on the note pad: giraffes at hotel—fed through window? I wondered if I got that one right, and decided to pay closer attention. Another call came in; I put the Baron on hold and told my old friend Beth that I'd call her back. My brother picked up where he'd left off. I soon had a page and a half of notes covering everything from the quality of cassava in the Lilongwe market, to what he'd learned from a Kenyan bar-tender about Mau Mau oaths.

As the Baron started to wind down, he suddenly remem-bered who he was talking to. "How're you feeling these days?"

My brother was aware, as were all of my friends and fam-ily, that I'd had a recent mastectomy and breast reconstruction, thanks to a very aggressive carcinoma, not to mention a close encounter with a murderer only months ago.

"A few scars here and there, Baron, but I'm almost back to normal."

"You always were the strong one, Tess. And really, you got-ta do this African trip. It's a once-in-a-lifetime opportunity."

He rang off before I had the chance to tell him what can-cer had taught me: everything is a once-in-a-lifetime opportu-nity, even the chance to tango with a pillow.

2

BIRD'S EYE VIEW

IF GOVERNMENT SPIES used seagulls for surveillance (are you sure they don't?), they'd observe two La Jolla teens steering shiny Segways along Mission Beach boardwalk, stopping at a weather-beaten surf shop for a drug connection. They'd see a young Chicano adding a burst of turquoise to an outdoor mural in National City. If the seagulls swooped at just the right moment, they'd notice that the new manatee at Sea World likes to chase his own fart bubbles. Later, as smog and dampness pressed down on the long summer evening, those same avian spies might watch my solid size 16 butt sliding into the driver's seat of my silver FX.

I'd been feeling betwixt and between, like Michael Moore without a cause, for a few weeks now. My employer, the software giant Imitech, had eliminated my job, along with many others, in a re-org designed to leave stockholders ecstatic and employees bent forward, grasping their ankles—business as usual in corporate America. But after cancer and two close encounters with murder, a job layoff hardly registered on my personal Richter scale. I had current database and web programming skills and a degree in math. When I returned my friend's phone call yesterday, a new paycheck possibility had emerged, so I wasn't too concerned about work.

What did sap my serotonin were Lana's future plans. As Lana and I had set about solving one of San Diego's most gruesome murders last Spring, we'd both met people we were attracted to. Lana's new fellow, a Feng Shui marketing exec, seemed like Mr. True Mensch. Maybe Mr. Right. The woman I'd met, an assistant music producer in L.A. named Nova, had had the good sense to cut and run when she realized my lifestyle frequently ran at Orange Alert.

I felt the satisfying engagement of the FX's gearshift as I backed out of my driveway. My humble home, with its chamois-colored stucco, birds of paradise, and purple passionflower vines, filled me with poignancy. A VA mortgage from my Navy service made the house purchase possible, but even with employment income, having a roommate was essential to keep the mortgage paid. It looked like Lana was on the fast track for marriage. Who else could I live with that would be so compatible? Lana and I had learned each other's habits, preferences, and hot buttons. Breaking in a new housemate would take time, and unlike employment, there were no prospects on the horizon. Besides, losing Lana would be more than losing a housemate, and I wasn't ready to head in that direction just yet.

Instead, I headed through the streets of my comfortable Mission Hills neighborhood. Breezes blew through screen doors and sprinklers spurted. Pigeons scattered in the queen palms. Dogs welcomed people home. Cats celebrated yet another personal Independence Day and eyed the pigeons. At University Avenue, I turned east into Hillcrest; caught every possible red light in the gnarly traffic; and at Sixth, headed north onto 163. With the help of my four-wheeled Silver Bullet, I zipped in and out of lanes, passing tentative tourists, and avoiding low riders who were high. San Diego traffic was beginning to rival L.A.'s, but the nimble Silver Bullet was up to the challenge. My left breast may have exited, stage right; my employer may have ditched my databases; my housemate might soon mate in another house; but damn it, my car could still cruise. At least that was something.

I took the 805 North exit, stayed in the far right lane, and followed the ramp east onto Balboa. I was meeting my friend Kari for burgers and a few games of pool at the Boll Weevil. The Weevil makes some of the best burgers in the city, and they serve them to you before they're cooked dry. In more ways than one, my life philosophy compels me to risk the rare *e coli* if it means tasting the juice.

I'd just pulled into the Weevil's parking lot off Convoy when Kari's RAV4 entered from the opposite direction. I walked over to greet her, noticing the colorful bumper sticker: "My child is a shining star at Sandburg Elementary."

Kari's yellow jersey top and white Capri pants showed off her tawny skin and taut figure. Instead of her usual dreadlocks, she wore buttercup and hot pink scrunchies in her unbraided hair. She looked pretty good for a woman who packed more responsibility and stress into her life than anyone has a right to. As a hate crimes sergeant with the San Diego police and the single mother of two, Kari certainly deserved whatever release a burger and a game of pool could provide.

I gave her a hug and gestured to the bumper sticker. "Looks like either Simone or Hunter inherited mom's brains."

"Definitely Simone. The day Hunter brings home a good report card is the day our city government will shine." In a city where 'mayoral election' is often a punch line, her comment brought a laugh.

Our eyes soon adjusted to the dim interior of the Weevil, with its dark slat ceiling and rusty farm implement decor. The yeast odor of a thousand beers smothered those of cow burger. A waitress right out of *Mel's Diner* led us to a table near the juke box, and slid two menus in front of us. "Can I get you ladies something to drink?"

"Corona with lime," I replied, and Kari seconded the notion. We got down to the serious business of choosing between temptations like A-One-Derful Burger, The Big Daddy, and Honey-Stung Fried Chicken.

Forty-five minutes later, my cholesterol was higher, the air smelled yeastier, Jewel crooned from the juke box, and I sank two stripes on the break. When I missed my next shot, Kari sank her orange, blue, and purple solids with downright elegance. She left me with an awkward shot: 10-ball in the corner pocket, with the 8-ball barely kissing it on the left. I leaned into the shot and tried to use about a quarter-tip of low left English. The shot went astray.

"These sticks are warped," I complained, as I finally exhaled. I enjoy shooting pool—its geometric lines and angles appeal to me—but my game was off this evening; I had a lot on my mind. I soon lost to Kari, and broke for stripes in our second game.

As I plotted a shot I knew I couldn't make, Kari sucked on the lime from her empty Corona and asked, "Heard from Lana?"

"Got a post card Tuesday. She and Gable are still at that lavender farm in Provençe, kicking back with some ex-pat friends of his." I signaled the waitress for two more brews. "Lana's Finnish, you know?" Kari nodded with minimal interest. "Somehow she managed to hook up with three Finnish tourists, out there in the French countryside. She and Gable invited them to dinner. I hope she doesn't come back with any experimental Finnish recipes."

The waitress delivered our Coronas. I tried a soft stroke with a bit of draw to execute a 12-15 combo, and keep the cue ball nearby. My shot worked; I'm good at soft stroking. "She and Gable were due back next Monday, but they extended their stay another week."

"Don't blame them. Sounds romantic." On her turn, Kari scratched. "While we're on romantic . . . Girl, how 'bout coming to my place tonight?"

Years ago, Kari and I had dated, but it hadn't worked. After that we'd traveled in different circles until fate drew me into two murder investigations, and her role as a police sergeant rekindled our friendship. With Lana in Europe and with no lover in my life, I'd taken to hanging out with Kari—a casual movie here, a few dances there. I should have known better; it was becoming obvious that she hoped for more than I could offer. Time to slow-roll the 9 ball in the corner pocket; time to break the news.

My shot rolled true. On the juke box, Wynonna Judd lamented a broken heart.

"I appreciate the offer," I began, "but I've got a big trip ahead of me tomorrow. I'm leaving town for a while." I sank the 11 ball and went two rails for tight position on the 14.

Kari put her cue stick on the ground and stood up straight. "You're *leavin' town*? What for?"

I pocketed the 14, then got over-confident and scratched. "Remember my friend Beth Butler? Back in '99, she left UCSD's Supercomputer Department to become CIO of a software firm in Albuquerque. You must've heard me mention her." Kari, spotting the cue ball, merely nodded. "Well, Beth called me yesterday and offered me temp contract work out there."

Kari sank her last solid, set herself up perfectly for the 8-ball, and won the game.

"I see my impending departure hasn't hurt your pool skills."

She tucked her cue stick into its holder along the wall and brushed blue chalk dust from the front of her yellow blouse. "Girl, you can be a real. . . ."

A hefty guy bumped into her on his way to the Men's Room, managing to turn the not-so-accidental contact into a salacious event. Kari, who had once been in an abusive marriage, has a very short fuse for that shit.

"B . . . ," he began, but she had the guy in a choke hold before he could "itch."

She flashed her badge. "I don't appreciate you coppin' a feel when you walk by." Our fellow Weevil customers looked anxious. Kari released her hold. "Get near us again and I'll book you for attempted assault."

He was soon gone with the whiz.

The interaction apparently helped dissipate any tension between us. We sipped our last Corona, and chatted about her kids. Eventually she asked, "So what kind of work has Beth got for you?"

"Her outfit nailed a government contract to data-mine pharmacies for purchases of cold and flu medicines. . . ."

"To see who's buying meth lab ingredients?"

"No, more like an early warning system for possible bioterror attacks. It's based on pattern recognition algorithms." Kari's expression told me the concept was still fuzzy. "If lots of people in an area suddenly experience flu-like symptoms, it might indicate a bioterrorist strike."

"Or ptomaine at the local salad bars." With the hand that

used to hold cigarettes when she was a smoker, Kari twisted the scrunchies in her hair.

"That's where my work comes in. I'll be refining a program that recognizes normal flu medicine purchase patterns. The software will be able to tell when a pattern is out of the ordinary."

Kari smiled. "I can't believe you, of all people, will be working for Homeland Security."

"Hey, I was once married to a guy who works for a top spook agency." I picked up a leftover French fry and munched it. "Besides, Beth's contract isn't with Homeland Security."

"Who else tries to detect bioterrorism?"

"Anti-terrorism's big business, Kari; every government contractor is after a piece of the pie. The government's got more creepy divisions and departments snooping and experimenting and researching, seducing our tax dollars and eroding our rights, than the average schmoe would believe possible. And unfortunately, as the daily news graphically demonstrates, we're still not really 'secure'."

"I thought the feds got organized after 9/11. Doesn't the Department of Homeland Security coordinate everything now?"

"Neither the FBI, NSA, nor the CIA is under Homeland Security. They all report to the Director of National Intelligence, in parallel with Homeland Security. The Department of Defense has been especially creative—almost all of their spook functions are hidden from both Homeland Security *and* DNI overview. You don't hear about DARPA or DIA or DSS much, do you? Or my favorite, the Defense Security Cooperation Agency? 'Cooperation'—what a joke! Federal turf battles are just like the ones you complain about at SDPD, only more expensive."

"But doesn't that mean a lot of duplicated effort and cost inefficiencies?"

"Give this woman a cigar! Believe me, the official right hand of homeland security doesn't know what the unofficial left hand is doing."

Kari shook her head in disbelief. We headed for the parking lot. "How long you gonna be gone?"

"Beth said the work should last a few weeks. They've already done the basics."

"Got someone to take care of the dogs until Lana gets back?"

"Remember my neighbor Smacker?"

"Good-lookin' kid about 20, sings rap, right?"

I nodded. "He'll take care of Raj and Pookie."

Kari unlocked the door of her RAV4 and turned to me. "Gonna miss you." The voice of this tough police sergeant sounded as shaky as James McGreevey's political future.

I hugged her long and tight. She felt good in my arms, smelled good, too. I began to reconsider her overnight invitation, but some high school punks at a nearby taco stand started yelling cat calls. I guess the sight of two women being that close for that long exceeded their hormonal tolerance levels. We broke the embrace. "I'll call when I get back in town."

"Keep your ass out of trouble, OK? I'm not gonna be there in New Mexico to help you out."

I waved good-bye and watched as her RAV4 bumped through the parking lot potholes and out onto the street.

Back home, I packed for the trip. I pressed my weight against one big suitcase to latch it. The suitcase was on my bed. Leaning on it brought me closer to the side of my double bed where no one sleeps, closer to the pillow I'd tangoed with. On a whim and a whoosh of loneliness, I decided to place an online personal ad. I booted up; navigated to Planet Out; uploaded a recent photo; and wrote:

> If you enjoy tearing the wings off butterflies; if you're only in the mood when your moon's in Pluto; or if you only communicate by satellite, move to the next ad. I'm an attractive GWF, late 40's, brown/brown, 5'5", size 16. I look a little like Isabella Rossellini, at least after I've had my coffee. Seeking educated, emotionally stable woman with sense of humor who's open to conversation, imagination, and osculation. (Look it up). Let's sit barefoot on my back patio, gaze at the stars, and tear the foil off a bottle of champagne.

I added information about my favorite movies, books, and activities, then saved the ad, shut down the computer, and got ready for bed. Big day ahead of me tomorrow, little dogs beside me tonight.